The Year
Mrs. Montague
Cried

by Susan White

2011
Acorn Press

ISBN 978-1-894838-57-3
All rights reserved.
Designed by Matt Reid

Printed in Canada by Transcontinental

Canada Council   Conseil des Arts
for the Arts   du Canada

The publisher acknowledges the support of the Government of Canada through the Canada Book Fund of the Department of Canadian Heritage for our publishing activities. We also acknowledge the support of the Canada Council for the Arts for our publishing program.

Library and Archives Canada Cataloguing in Publication

White, Susan, 1956-
The year Mrs. Montague cried / Susan White.
ISBN 978-1-894838-57-3

I. Title.
PS8645.H5467Y42 2011   jC813'.6   C2011-901662-1

ACⓄRNPRESS

P.O. Box 22024
Charlottetown, Prince Edward Island
C1A 9J2
acornpresscanada.com

To Zac who stood in the doorway of my writing room and said that he would hold a book of mine someday. Sadly, he will not hold this one but it holds him, just as my heart always will.

Thanks to the WFNS and the 33rd
Atlantic Writing Competition.

Thanks to Terrilee and Acorn Press
for believing in this story.

Thanks to Elizabeth Peirce
for the first stages of editing.

Special thanks to Caitlin Drake
for all her guidance and expertise.

Thanks to Wendy Harris for helping
with medical details. Any mistakes or
inconsistencies are mine, not hers.

I acknowledge and am so grateful for the
influence and support of the following people.
Their love and example planted the seeds
and helped this story grow.

Tim and Colleen who lost their precious
Lindsay to Neuroblastoma

Taylor, Anne, Holly, Victoria, Thomas
and all the other kids who were really there
the year that "Mrs. Montague" cried

Kathy for being in the classroom next door

Ruth for always being there
with her office door open

Alice for making me laugh
and letting me cry

Marlene, Kim and Louisa for getting
me through those first days and months

Karen for reading the newspaper and being the
kind of wonderful friend that pays attention

To my Mom and Dad who taught me so
beautifully how to be a parent.

To my amazing kids Megan, Chapin and Caleb
and their loves Cody, Brianne and Ashlie.

To my husband Burton who has always believed
in me. Together, we have been blessed with
creating a love, a life and a family that endures.

"Teaching is leaving a vestige of oneself in the development of another. And surely the student is a bank where you can deposit your most precious treasures."

– Eugene P. Bertin

"Educating the mind without educating the heart is no education at all."

– Aristotle

"Teaching is a daily exercise in vulnerability."

– Parker Palmer

My Journal
Taylor Anne Broderson
September 2002
Grade Four
Mrs. Montague's Class

September 3

It's not that I really hate the first day of school as much as it is that I hate what I have to give up when school starts. It seems at first like it is no big deal. In those first few days of September you believe that you will still be able to fit all the things you love to do into that space between after school and school-night bedtime. You really think things won't change so quickly, but they al-ways do. Homework and all those other everyday things start to take up your time and before the leaves have finished turning on the maple trees, it feels like you've been in school forever.

This year, I think the hardest thing to give up will be the lake.

Corey finally learned to swim well enough to get out to the raft, so this summer instead of Mom sitting on the shore while we swam in close, she swam out with us and we would swim off of the raft all afternoon. Lying on that raft waiting for the water to drip off my bathing suit and letting the heat of the sun convince me to jump into the cool water again is one of my one million most favourite things about summer. (We don't have enough journal time to write about all the other 999,999, so I'll see how many I can list before Mrs. Montague tells us to stop writing.)

My 1,000,000 most favourite things about summer:

1. *the lake*
2. *burnt marshmallows*
3. *camping*
4. *sleeping in*
5. *strawberry shortcake*
6. *screen doors creaking*
7. *driving over the Confederation Bridge, trying to keep my eyes closed the whole time*
8. *mussels and lobster at Aunt Rachel's cottage*
9. *buttercups*
10. *fireflies*

September 4

I didn't finish my list yesterday, but I don't feel like continuing it right now. We write in our journals almost every day. Mrs. Montague tells us to write whatever we are thinking about. "Just write," she says. This is my second year with Mrs. Montague. I had her in Grade Three and this year she is teaching Grade Four and I was lucky enough to get her again. My Grade Three journal is pretty stupid though. My spelling was bad and I wrote really dumb stuff. I wanted to throw it away when I was cleaning out my desk at the end of the year, but I remembered Mrs. Montague always told us to keep our journal because someday she said they will mean a lot to us when we look back and read the things we thought about when we were in Grade Three. I don't really think I want to remember what a dork I was, but when I took it home I got Mom to put it somewhere, wherever that somewhere is that she puts all our other dorky stuff that is supposedly going to be so valuable to us some day.

We didn't have Mrs. Montague for May and June. Her son died. He was in a car accident. He died on a weekend and Mrs. Montague didn't come back to school on Monday. We had Miss Flynn for the rest of the year. She was really nice, but we all missed Mrs. Montague. Mrs. Montague doesn't read our journals. She just looks over our shoulders to see if we're writing. Most days she asks us if we want to share what we have written. She writes, too. I like it when she reads us her writing.

September 5

Mrs. Montague tells us to read back what we wrote the day before. She says that all the time and she always says, "Just write." She just said that to Thomas a couple of minutes ago when he was whining that he couldn't think of anything to write about. When we are finished writing she asks us if we want to share our journals with the class. If we want to, we can read all or part of what we have written. Maggie always shares. She uses journal as her major suck-up time. I could do that if I wanted to. I could describe this autumn day using descriptive phrases that would capture the audience, and blah, blah, blah. I could write about the classroom rules and the value of de-mocracy. But I am not Maggie Worden. I am Taylor Anne Broderson and I just write.

I was at Grammie's the morning after Mrs. Mon-tague's son died. Mom and Dad had gone to Uncle Paul's birthday party the night before and Corey and I stayed at Grammie's. Mom called me that morning and as soon as I heard her voice I knew something was wrong. She told me that she had some bad news. She told me that Mrs. Montague's son Zachary had been killed in a car accident. Mom was crying. I don't remember what I said. But all day I just kept thinking about Mrs. Montague. I hope she doesn't see what I am writing when she walks by. I don't want to make her sad. I knew she wouldn't come to school that Monday. There would have to be a funeral and everything. Mom and Dad went to Hampton to the funeral home. They said that there were a lot of people there. Mom wouldn't let me go. Dad gave me the death talk before they left. He gave me that same talk when our dog Bud got hit by a car. "Everything and everybody dies," he said. I'm not three. I know that. I told Mom to tell Mrs. Montague we missed her. It was so weird at school that Monday. All the teachers were quiet. Mr. Caines came and talked to us. A lot of us cried that day.

September 6

Bill opened the bus door for me and Corey this morning and helped me lift my backpack up the stairs. We are his first stop in the morning so we get to pick any seat we want. I don't even try to take a back seat. The high school kids would just throw me out of it, and Bill doesn't notice anything they do unless there is smoke involved.

Writing is my favourite part of school. I won the

writing contest last year. It was during Canadian Book Week. The assembly to give out the prizes was the Friday after Mrs. Montague's son died. In writing class the Friday before, she told me to work more on my ending. I worked all during class and up until bedtime that night trying to get it just right. I revised and revised but I wanted to show it to Mrs. Montague before I did my good copy. I am writing her name a lot. I think I'll use Mrs. M. for short. I suppose that doesn't really belong in this paragraph.

I didn't get to show it to her. Mrs. Montague, I mean Mrs. M., called me at home to congratulate me. I didn't know what to say when I heard her voice on the phone. I said, "Thank you." After I got off the phone I thought that I should have said something about Zachary. I should have said I was sorry or asked her how she was doing. I didn't say anything, just, "Thank you."

September 9

Zachary's funeral was right after school. The teachers put us on the buses early so that they could go. The bus was so quiet. Hardly anyone talked. Mr. Caines waved from the front step to tell the buses to go. Bill's bus goes right by the church where the funeral was and when we drove down the hill all you could see were cars lined up on both sides of the road. He drove very slowly and some kids put the windows down. It was a really hot afternoon. The lawn and all around the church door was packed with people, mostly teenagers, but it was so quiet. The funeral car was parked close to the road. The sun glared off the side windows. All the way home, even when the noise level got pretty much back to normal, I kept thinking about that long black car.

Mom took us to the lake after school yesterday. When we got there, I tried really hard to pay attention to every detail of that swim. I felt the rocks and mud under my bare feet as I walked slowly into the water. I went out as far as I could walk so that the cold water was right up to my chin. Then I ducked under and held my breath as long as I could. When I surfaced, I swam to the raft, climbed the ladder, and stood with my arms stretched out looking at the sky. It was a deep blue with only a few clouds. I listened hard to all the sounds around me: the birds, the rustle of the leaves, and the lapping of the waves. I thought this is the lake I love. It felt kind of church-like and I stayed that way until Corey got up on the raft beside me. He jumped at me and pushed me in the water, making me swallow half the lake. I was really mad. Mom hollered at him and told him not to do that again. He almost wrecked my last swim of the summer. I swam a long way from the raft and pretended I was all alone, all alone in my lake. Alone, with no little brother who wrecks everything. I floated on my back until Mom yelled that it was time to go.

September 10

It is really hot out today. I wish I was at the lake.

Mrs. M. hasn't read us anything from her journal yet. Last year she always read us what she wrote and she always told us stories about her kids. She has, I mean, she had four kids, three boys and a girl. Almost every day in her journal she would write something about at least one of them.

She said Zac's name yesterday. She started to tell us something, but then she stopped. She turned toward her desk and told us to get our math books out.

Mrs. M. has a picture of her kids on her desk. They are all standing on the side of a road at a place called the Great Divide. Mrs. M. is holding that picture right now. She is staring at it. I write a couple of words and then I look back up at her. She just keeps staring at it. Some of the kids around me have stopped writing. Luke is drawing army men on a piece of scrap paper. Kayla just passed a note to Holly. They don't seem to see what I see. I just keep looking at Mrs. M. holding that picture. It makes me want to cry.

September 11

  Mrs. Ashe is here. She came in a few minutes ago and told us to get our journals out until the supply teacher arrives. Mrs. M. just went home. I was the first one in the room this morning. Every morning Mrs. M. is standing at the door when we come from our lockers but she wasn't this morning. I heard the sound just before I came into the room, but I wasn't sure what it was. It sounded a bit like laughing, but when I saw Mrs. M. at her desk I knew she was not laughing. She had her head down and her hands were over her face. I stood in the doorway and didn't know what to do. Other kids were coming in behind me, and I felt like I wanted to protect her, to tell them not to come in. I wanted to go over to her, but I didn't know what to say. I stood there frozen. She looked up at me and asked me to go get Mrs. Ashe. By that time the room was full of kids. Mrs. M. always greets us with "Good morning—put your homework books in the tub and put your indoor shoes on." Her words are like a motor that starts us every morning. Without her words, it seemed like we were stalled. All of us were just standing there not moving as our teacher sobbed. She looked up at me again and I went to get Mrs. Ashe. I don't remember what I said to her, but she went right over to our classroom. She put her arms around Mrs. M. We sat at our desks with our eyes down as they stood there. There was no sound in the room but Mrs. Montague's crying and Mrs. Ashe quietly telling her to go home. After she left, the noise crept up slowly but no one said a word about any of it.

September 12

Today is my Dad's birthday. He is forty-three years old. Mom is having a surprise party for him but it won't be any surprise. Mom always has a corn boil on the weekend closest to Dad's birthday. The surprise will be if she remembers to invite anybody. Dad usually ends up inviting people himself. This year Corey and I get to stay home. I'm not sure why. We usually have to go to Grammie's.

Mrs. M. is back today. She looks all right. When I came in I wanted to say something. Coming down the hall I thought that if she was standing in the doorway I would ask her if she was feeling better.

But she hadn't been sick so that sounded dumb. Then I thought I would ask, "How are you doing?" No, how about, "I'm glad you're not crying." Real bright! I ended up not saying one thing, not one thing. Holly came right behind me and said, "It's nice to see you back." That would have been a good thing to say, but not right after someone else just said it.

IT'S NICE TO SEE YOU BACK, MRS. MONTAGUE. Maybe she'll see that when she looks over my shoulder.

September 16

Somebody did the inviting. Our house was crawling with people. They came in droves. I love that word, droves. I got to stay up until 11:00. After I went to bed I lay there and heard all the noise downstairs. It was a racket. That's my Mom's word, racket. When she uses it I always think of Corey and me pinging the badminton birdie across the net at Aunt Rachel's cottage. What a racket!

We are getting our school pictures done today. Last year I forgot about it being picture day and I had on a green shirt, which was the same colour as the fake trees in the background the photographer was using. From across the room my picture looked like a head and arms sticking out of a big pine tree, like someone stuck in a Christmas tree.

I answered the classroom door one time last year and Mrs. M.'s son was standing there. I looked up. He was very tall. Mrs. M. gave him her car keys and told him to be careful. That sounded just like my Mom. Be careful, she always says. Even when I just bike to the end of the driveway she says be careful. Be careful or be good. Dad says be good when I'm going up to bed. How bad can I be in bed?

September 17

I didn't write much yesterday about the party. Corey and I got to keep the money from the beer bottles. We split it. Mom said that Uncle Paul contributed the most. I woke up sometime in the night and heard Dad yelling. I couldn't tell at first what was going on, but then I heard, "You're not driving, Paul. You can stay here tonight." He was on the couch when we got up in the morning and Corey and I watched the Inspector Gadget movie for about the fiftieth time, while Uncle Paul snored and groaned. There was a lot of food left over. Two bags of Party Mix. Corey separates everything in Party Mix. It is weird. He makes piles of pretzels, cheese things, Ringolos, and those flat things before he starts to eat. Then he eats one at a time in order, one of each, and then starts over. He freaks right out if you take one or if you mix them up on him.

Mrs. M. is reading *Danny, the Champion of the World* to the class. Read Aloud is my second most favourite part of the day. Actually it is my third most favourite. First is S.S.R. which means Sustained (we keep at it for twenty minutes) Silent (the part Thomas doesn't get) Reading (of course). Second is writing class and then comes Read Aloud. Mrs. M. picks really good books and reads to us every day. Victoria told me that last year Mrs. Sharp started reading them Charlotte's Web in September and didn't finish it until March. Then she told them that she didn't have time to finish another book, so never read to them again for the rest of the year.

Last year when Mrs. M. read a part in a book that made her think of something that had happened in her own life, she always stopped reading and told us a story. One day Thomas said, "You have a story for everything, Mrs. Montague." She laughed and told us that we all have stories to tell. When we tell our stories we let other people see us and when they see us, they see themselves. Today for the first time this year, she stopped reading and started to tell us a story. But she had only said a few words when she stopped. Tears started dripping down her cheeks and she turned away. She walked over to her desk and got a Kleenex. She came back and started reading the book again. Nobody asked her to finish her story.

I love the picture in the front of the book that shows Danny as a baby. He is naked. Nude, bare, buff, birthday suit. The thesaurus wasn't much help for this one. It said "unadorned," whatever that means. Bare-assed, Dad would say. That's what Danny was in the picture and everybody laughed when Mrs. M. held it up. But who doesn't have a picture like that around somewhere? Parents seem to like to take pictures of their unadorned children. It gives them something to embarrass their kids with later.

September 18

"Look at all the little Zacharys." I read back what I wrote yesterday and it reminded me of the story Mrs. M. told us one day last year. Her daughter had come to the door for something and Nick said, "All your kids look alike." She told us about going to pick up Zac at camp one day. He ran over to where she was parked and a few kids ran over with him. One of the boys looked in the window and hollered. "Look at all the little Zacharys."

I don't think anyone would say, "Look at the little Taylor," if they saw Corey for the first time. He doesn't look anything like me. He doesn't act anything like me either. His whining, sniveling, pouting, big baby routine has a place of its own in the Broderson household. I wouldn't get away with the "I can't do anything myself," "I'm too tired," "I can't carry my own book bag," "I'm pathetic," act. It would land me a 7:00 bedtime or a kick in the rear end. But not little Corey, Mommy's precious baby.

Mom talked to Aunt Rachel for a long time on the phone last night. They seemed to be talking about baby Corey the whole time. What am I, chopped liver? Anyway it was all about Corey. He isn't eating, he isn't sleeping, he isn't riding his bike, and he isn't human. Oh wait, that's just my opinion. I haven't figured out what he is yet.

September 19

Holly went home sick at recess time. She puked on the bus. Kayla was sitting with her and should really get an A+ for her use of descriptive phrases when retelling it. Did we need to know about each chunk? New paragraph or I'll be sick, too.

I got my math test back this morning. I did

pretty well. Thomas the Brain got his test all right. I won't hear the end of that for a while. Maggie will probably share today. I can see it coming. She'll be all geared up about the importance of learning from our mistakes, trying our best, and how it doesn't matter what mark you get because everyone learns differently. Really what she'd like to write is that she could spit because my mark is higher than hers.

September 20

Corey is home sick today. He didn't even get up, let alone get dressed and try to eat breakfast. He didn't throw up either. He just stayed in bed whining and he got to stay home.

It is raining. Indoor recess. I think I'll work on my story, "Mystery at Cabin Cove." Mrs. M. conferenced me yesterday and said that I needed to pull it together and give it an ending. To conference us, Mrs. M. sits with us on the couch. We read her our piece of writing and she tells us what we need to do to make it better. When she thinks it is done she tells us to do a good copy and it gets published in our class book. No one is allowed to come near during a conference. She says it is her office and pretends that there is a wall around the couch. We know it's not a real office, but we all act

like it is and wait by the pretend door for our turn
to meet with Mrs. M.

Endings I could use:

1. They all lived happily ever after.

2. Everybody died.

3. The princess married the handsome prince.

4. She turned into a toad.

5. The city blew up.

6. She woke up.

7. The fairy godmother came.

8. She rubbed a magic bottle.

9. All her dreams came true.

10. She goes to jail.

   The first one has really been overdone. I am
going to try to list ten more story endings before
journal time is over.

1. The aliens came back for her.

2. She got a dog.

3. Her brother grew up.

4. Her brother threw up.

5. It was always summer.

6. They found her alive on a deserted island.

7. The bell rang.

8. The dog ate it.

Mrs. M. told us to stop writing but I need two more.

9. She didn't wake up.
10. Nobody died.

I kind of cheated on those last two.

September 23

I wrote the ending for my story and it was none of the endings I listed on Friday. I made it so that Rosalind (my main character) doesn't find out for sure who left the box of shells on the picnic table. She thinks it was the girl from the next cottage and hopes that next summer they can become friends. I left it that way so maybe I could write a sequel. I like that word sequel. Mrs. M. said that I did a good job telling the story and that my ending left the reader thinking. She says good writing makes the reader think.

September 25

Mr. Caines came after recess and read to us. He was standing at the door when we came in. He asked me where the book was for Read Aloud. He sat at Mrs. Montague's desk and read. I wasn't listening. I didn't hear one thing he read. That's not true. I did hear him read the part about Danny

getting caught cheating. Mr. Caines used a boom-
ing voice with an English accent when he read
Captain Lancaster's part and a squeaky pathetic
voice for Danny. But other than that I was mostly
wondering if Mrs. M. had gone home. She had
seemed OK before recess. I even saw her smiling
and laughing in the hall with Mrs. Ashe. Maybe
she had taken sick. A headache maybe or maybe
she threw up. She hadn't looked sick. Mr. Caines
kept reading and everybody seemed to be listening and acting like this was perfectly normal. Like
our teacher just disappeared from time to time
and principals with hidden dramatic talents came
along and took her place. Then she walked in.
She leaned on the ledge at the back of the room
and waited for Mr. Caines to finish the part he
was reading. When he was done she walked up
and thanked him. He passed her the book and left
without saying anything. She put the bookmark in
and told us to get our math books out.

September 26

Everybody died. That would be an ending that
pulls everything together. Everybody died. Everybody was gone. Nobody was there anymore.
Anymore. No more. I'm stuck on that. No more.
My Grampie died when I was six. He is no more. I

see his picture in a gold frame on top of the piano at Grammie's, and I remember him a bit when I really try. Mrs. Montague's son is no more. No more. When people die there is no more of them. If my Mom died there would be no more of her. If I died there would be no more of me. I don't like what I'm writing today. If I had enough white-out I would white this all out. I'm going to stop writing about it and write about something happier.

Corey got in big trouble last night. He was whining about clearing off the table and Dad lost it. He started moving though when Dad came up behind him. Corey had to finish the table by himself and load the dishwasher alone. I guess Dad is getting as tired of Corey's sniveling as I am.

October

October 1

Mrs. M's son was twenty. He had a red and white truck. I saw him drive by one day when I was at Victoria's house.

My October writing goal is to use the dictionary and a thesaurus more.

We are going on a class trip to Elmhurst Outdoors on Friday. Mom is going to drive and I get to choose two kids to drive with us. The two kids I choose, desire, wish, kill for, give one's right arm for, take a fancy to, have one's eye on, lean toward, have designs on, wish to goodness, prefer, favour for Mom to drive to Elmhurst Outdoors are

1. Victoria
2. Holly, if she doesn't bug me too much in the next two days
3. Adrianna would be my third choice if I had to choose someone else.

We finished *Danny* today. I told Mom she should read it to Corey, but then I thought if she did, he would already know the story when he gets in Mrs. Montague's class. I really like most of the books that Mrs. M. reads to us. Mrs. M. started another book today. It is called *Matilda* and was written by Roald Dahl. He wrote *Danny, the Champion of the World*, too, but *Matilda* is nothing like it.

October 15

Long weekends. I love them. I love the feeling on the Sunday night when you know that there is no school the next day. We both got to stay up past 10:00 Sunday night because we were late getting home from Grammie's. We had a huge turkey dinner at suppertime.

Corey was so annoying yesterday. He cried about everything. He started on the drive to Grammie's. All I did was pinch him a couple of times. You would think I had zapped him with a thousand volts of electricity. He fell asleep partway there and stayed asleep in the car in Grammie's driveway for at least an hour. That gave me some peace and quiet, but he made up for it when he woke up. He cried forever. He hasn't done that since he was a baby. Oh what am I saying? He still is a baby.

October 16

Thank goodness Wednesday is pizza day. Grammie sent the leftover turkey home with Mom. So it's been back-to-back turkey meals.

Dad brought the raft in last night. He rowed out and pulled up the anchor and hauled it in. I wanted to go out with him, but Mom wouldn't let me. She didn't want Corey to ask to go so she wouldn't let me. I hate that everything I do Corey has to do too, and that I'm not allowed to do anything that he can't do. I am older and should have some special considerations. I waded out though and helped Dad pull the raft up on the shore. Corey didn't even try to help. Lazy, whiny, wimpy. Need I go on with the adjectives that describe my little brother?

October 17

Mrs. M. read her journal entry to us yesterday. The first bit was about turkey sandwiches. Isn't that funny that we both were thinking about our lunches and turkey? She read about her family going to Kings Landing on Thanksgiving and eating at the King's Head Inn. They have been going there for seventeen years. Tears were streaming down her cheeks as she read, "This year Zac was not with us. He did not walk along the path where last year he walked, with Caleb on his shoulders, pretending that he was going to pitch him over the railing into the river." She read on and I didn't know if she would be able to finish. Her husband bought a very large wooden spoon at the gift shop and she kept reading about what each of her other kids had done and didn't mention Zac again.

October 18

Friday. I am so glad. I know we only had school four days this week, but it seemed really long. Corey has been up through the night almost every night this week. He wakes up crying so loudly that we all wake up. Mom gets up with him, but I can't get back to sleep until he settles down and Mom turns out the hall light again. I am going to Grammie's for the night. She is going to pick me up after school because Mom is taking Corey to the doctor. Dad doesn't really like it when I drive with Grammie. He says she takes her half of the road in the middle. We will probably stop at the Co-op on the way to her house and she will buy whatever I ask her for.

A list of all the things I could ask for:

1. cheezies
2. coke
3. root beer
4. orange crush
5. waffles
6. fruit roll-ups
7. marshmallow fluff
8. pizza pockets
9. all the kinds of ice cream I like
10. an Archie comic book

I can't think of anything else. Last night when I was awake waiting for Brat-Face to stop crying, I randomly opened to pages in the Sears Wish Book and picked one thing off each page. On some of the pages it was really hard to decide. I opened to the underwear page, closed it, and picked again. What would I do with a bra? I picked Dad out a really big snow blower off of one page.

There is a big bruise on Corey's leg where I pinched him. I didn't even pinch hard.

October 21

I am almost finished Book 2 in *A Series of Unfortunate Events*. It is called *The Reptile Room*. I am going to write my own list of series of unfortunate events.

My Series of Unfortunate Events:

Corey was born
They brought him home from the hospital
He learned to walk
He learned to talk
He learned how to bug me

Another Series of Unfortunate Events:

My Grampie died
Mrs. Montague's son died
People died in New York on 9/11
My dog Bud was hit by a car
Danny's mother died (in the book)

October 22

Mrs. M. is in a really bad mood today. She just hollered at Justin Morrison. I almost fell off my chair it scared me so much. She never hollers. I don't know what Justin was doing but I'm really glad it wasn't me. She is writing like mad. Her head is down and there isn't a sound in this class-room. Everyone is writing in their journals or at least pretending to. She has not smiled all day and we didn't have Read Aloud after recess like we usually do. As soon as we came in she told us to get our journals out. When Holly asked why we weren't having Read Aloud, Mrs. M. just raised her voice and repeated, "Get your journals out."

I know all about bad moods these days. Mom and Dad have both been really crabby lately. When Dad picked me up from Grammie's Sunday morning, he said that Mom was really tired and that Corey was sick. He told me to help Mom, be good, and not to bug Corey.

Corey has been home all week. Dr. Henderson said he has the flu. He seemed OK to me last night when Mom gave him the last piece of my favourite dessert. Mom said he hasn't eaten enough to keep a bird alive in the last few days and he could have anything he wanted. What else is new?

Mrs. M. has her hands over her face. She is sit-ting so still with her head down, and her hands are completely covering her face. I feel weird. It is so quiet and I'm hot. I wish the fire alarm would go off or something. Maybe I should drop a book, pretend to choke, or fall out of my seat for real. I wish something would break the silence so that I don't have to look at her sitting there.

List of ten loud things:

1. Mr. McKay's voice
2. the train by Uncle Paul's house
3. the fire alarm
4. Maggie screaming like a girl
5. Grade Eight kids in the library
6. Corey crying in the middle of the night
7. Dad's Grateful Dead CD when Mom's not in the car
8. the cafeteria on Fridays
9. Thomas's stupid watch
10. silence

October 23

Mrs. Scott is our teacher today. We finished our spelling lesson early, so she is letting us write in our journals until recess time. I like it when Mrs. Scott comes. She always reads us ghost stories. Mom says she had her for a supply teacher when she was in school. She read ghost stories then, too. I am going to try and write a ghost story. I hope we have writing class today. Most of the time supply teachers don't have writing class. They think that no one will write.

October 24

I started my ghost story at home last night and will get Mrs. M. to conference me on what I have written so far. I hope she has some suggestions on how I can get the reader to see the ghost when none of the characters can see him. You can't see ghosts in the mirror, you know. You feel ghosts, I guess. How will my character feel the ghost? Maybe my ghost will move things or open and shut things. Maybe my ghost will make noises. He could make noises like Corey makes when he wakes up in the night. Moaning, groaning, pathetic noises. No, I want my ghost to be a good ghost that helps my character solve some problem.

I have a title. It seems I can always come up with a title, but it's getting the story worked out that gives me trouble. The title is "The Sawmill Ghost." This kid gets killed at the sawmill because a bad man that owns another mill rigs the saw so that it will break and people will come to his sawmill. The boy's best friend's father gets blamed and the kid comes back as a ghost trying to let the village know what really happened. The boy comes to be known as the Sawmill Ghost. I think somehow I'll make it so that the bad guy gets killed at the end.

October 25

I know it is not always the bad guy that dies. Mrs. M. helped me a lot with my story. I really like the first part I wrote that tells about the boy getting killed. His name is Nathanial. I didn't make it really gory but I did tell about all the blood.

I know exactly where Mrs. Montague's son died. It was on the road to Hampton. I always know when I am coming to it. The Smiths' mailbox is on one side and on the other side is a yellow arrow sign. There is a huge rock on the side of the road then a straight part. Dad says Zachary wasn't wearing his seatbelt and that he was thrown from his truck. He died right in the Walkers' front yard. That would be awful to have someone die in your front yard. He broke his neck. I don't know if a broken neck bleeds.

October 28

Mom and Corey are at the hospital today. They went to the doctor again yesterday, and today Corey has to have a whole bunch of tests. He will probably get to go to Dairy Queen on the way home. Mom is letting him eat whatever he wants lately. He got to buy a bag of Snickers bars yesterday and he only had to give me one.

Holly and I were on peer helper duty on the primary playground. We had to help one little girl because she went up the slide and was afraid to slide down. Holly went up and slid down with her. Kindergarten kids are wimps. Except for that kid named Brodie. He's not afraid of anything.

Ten things most kindergarten kids are afraid of:

1. a flea
2. their shadows
3. Mr. McKay
4. peeing their pants
5. the big kids on the bus
6. fire drills
7. Brodie
8. going out on the playground
9. coming in off the playground
10. the cafeteria

October 29

I cried last night. Nobody knows that and I don't know why I just wrote it down. Big deal, I cried. I laughed last night. There, it's balanced. In math class yesterday we learned about mass and balance. We had to put weights on one side then find things in the room that we thought would weigh the same so the scale would be balanced. Thomas thought his sneaker would weigh ten grams. His brain would weigh ten grams.

I have to figure out what I'm going to be for Halloween. I am going to go out with Holly and Adrianna. Adrianna's Dad is going to drive us.

Mrs. M. finished reading *Matilda* yesterday. It had a happy ending. She started reading *Because of Winn Dixie* to us today. In the book the girl's last name is Buloni, which is pronounced like the meat, bologna, which is not pronounced like it looks. The dictionary also says that Bologna is a city in Italy.

October 30

Mrs. M. asked us today what we were wearing for our Halloween costumes. Most of the kids don't know yet. They are probably like me and will throw something together at the last minute. She told us about a costume she made for Zac one year. He was in Beavers, and he was all excited about his party. From a picture in a magazine she got the idea to dress him up as a red cardboard thing of McDonald's French fries. She said it looked really cute in the magazine, but in reality it was a disaster. She got red Bristol board and made the container. She painted the golden arches and used string to tie the costume on over his shoulders. She cut big French fries from a brownish piece of foam. He looked adorable. But he couldn't walk, he couldn't sit, and he couldn't move to defend himself when Stephen Richard started pulling out the French fries and hitting Zac over the head with them. Some of the other kids joined in and Zac stood in the middle of the Legion hall and cried. Mrs. M. said she walked over and took off the Bristol board, picked up the fries, and vowed to never make another cutesy Halloween costume. She said after that, her kids usually just dressed up as army men. They probably felt less vulnerable with camouflage and helmets.

She told that whole story without a quiver. She laughed and smiled. I hope this means we will be getting more stories from her. Last year Justin said he liked the stories because it took up time and we would have to do less work. I just really like the stories.

I know who Stephen Richard is. His sister used to babysit Holly and her brother. I wonder if he remembers hitting Zachary over the head with foam French fries. I wonder if he is sorry, now that Zachary is dead.

November

November 1

We didn't write in our journals yesterday because we had a Halloween party. We didn't dress up but we did UNICEF activities and had some vegetables and dip. It is all about the healthy snacks now. The primary kids dressed up, and paraded through our room. Corey was a pirate. I suggested the McDonald's French fry thing but Mom just laughed. I would love to hit him over the head with a French fry or two.

Everybody has lots of junk in their lunches today. Mrs. Millett was on duty in the cafeteria and walked around making sure everyone ate their sandwiches first.

Inventory list of my Halloween loot or booty (a good pirate word):

Cans of pop: 6
Chips: 31 bags
Cheesies: 14 bags

Apples: 7 (Mom takes them)
Mini chocolate bars: 48
Smarties: 16
Glosette Peanuts: 11
Glosette Raisins: 9
Raisins: 2 (from the same house)
Suckers: 8
Candy kisses: 20
Candy apples: 1 (Our neighbour Mrs. Brown always makes us one. We eat it as soon as we get home. Mom picked mine up because Adrianna's Dad didn't go there and besides she doesn't make them for everyone.)

Anyone reading this might think I made my inventory up because who knows how many of everything they get at Halloween. Well I do. I sort everything and count it. I write it down and keep the list with me at all times. I keep track and mark off what I eat. Little brothers can't be trusted. Parents can't be trusted either, and Mom is home alone all day with that pillowcase full of temptation.

November 4

On Friday afternoon some high school kids came to do chemistry demonstrations. We each got a bag of gooey, Silly Putty stuff that they made with a bunch of chemicals.

We had a really long writing class today. This morning everyone had to say what their writing goal for November was, which took quite a while. My writing goal for November is to write some non-fiction pieces and to Google information that I want to write about. I googled Silly Putty last night. More than three hundred million eggs of Silly Putty have been sold since 1950. I read that fact to Mrs. M. She told me she was born in 1956. She said she got in trouble one time because she used the money her mother had given her for her brother's Christmas present to buy herself some Silly Putty. The Apollo 8 astronauts took Silly Putty to the moon with them. Did they play with it?

Corey has to pee in a bottle every time he goes to the bathroom, for twenty-four hours. He started last night after supper and is staying home today so Mom can get his pee all day. Mom has to take Corey's bottle to Dr. Henderson's office tomorrow morning. They have to do some kind of test on it.

Mrs. M. read a story today that she wrote. It was called "Runaway Rosie." She read us the title and the beginning sentence first. Her lesson today was on beginning sentences. After that, half the class picked "writing strong beginning sentences" as their November writing goal. Where's the imagination in that? Maggie went on painfully about how she has been struggling with her beginning sentences. Oh shut up! It's the rest of us struggling with her beginning, middle, ending, and every sentence she writes. They make us want to puke.

November 5

Taylor Anne! My Mom calls me Taylor Anne when she is mad at me. She screamed it last night and all I did was ask, "Why do I have to load the dishwasher when it is Corey's turn?" She just flipped out at me. Corey had been home all day. He hadn't picked up his Lego, which covered the family room floor. He was lying on the couch sleeping when I got home, and I couldn't play my music. He didn't have to eat his carrots, and he barely took a bite of his supper. Then he started bawling when Dad told him to start loading the dishwasher. After Mom screamed at me she went to her room, Corey went on the computer, and Dad helped me clean up. We didn't say a word to each other and I could hear Mom crying the whole time. When I was done I went out on my bike and rode all the way to the lake. I threw about a thousand rocks into the water and waited until almost bedtime to head home.

November 6

Today is Corey's seventh birthday. Grammie is coming for Corey's birthday supper. He asked for Zoodles, blueberry pancakes, and Pogo Sticks. That kid is so weird. Mom will have regular stuff, too, because I'm sure Grammie would not be too thrilled with the menu.

I found out that the Apollo 8 astronauts took Silly Putty with them to alleviate boredom and to fasten down items in a weightless environment. "Alleviate" means relieve or lessen. I don't think Silly Putty would alleviate, relieve, or lessen my boredom for very long. You can't do that much with it. It wouldn't even bounce in space, I don't think.

Ten things I would take to space to alleviate boredom:

1. Books 3 and 4 in A Series of Unfortunate Events
2. my Game Boy
3. my Sudoku books
4. my journal
5. a Rubik's cube
6. my 1001 Brain Teasers book
7. a deck of cards
8. my Stormy Seas game
9. my whole collection of Archie comics

I can't think of the tenth thing. I don't know if you can watch TV in space. A movie maybe. You can play DVDs on the Play Station. I could take the Play Station. Maybe I would take knitting needles and yarn. Grammie taught me how to knit dish-cloths. I am almost finished one and it doesn't look too bad.

10. knitting needles and yarn

November 7

Corey didn't eat any supper, not even a piece of his birthday cake. Mom didn't make him come to the table. Grammie and Mom talked about Corey almost the whole time. When they were having their tea they started talking about the hospital stuff. Dad made me leave the kitchen. He came outside with me and we just sat in the car until Grammie came out, and then we drove her home.

Erno Rubik invented the Rubik's cube. I love that name, Erno. I am going to use that name in the next story I write. I think Erno will be a dog. There are 1,790,000 sites online that talk about the Rubik's cube in some way. I read through one site and got to a section called "Permutations." The dictionary says that "permutation" means complete rearrangement. The number of permutations you can have with a Rubik's cube is a twenty-digit number. I didn't even try to read it. One site said that sheets of coloured stickers were sold so that people could cheat. They could peel off the coloured squares and put the stickers on so that it would look like they solved the whole puzzle. That is such a Thomas thing to do.

November 8

Mrs. M. started a new Read Aloud today. *There's a Boy in the Girls' Bathroom* is the title of the book. The boys have been really annoying all day. They keep hollering the title when they walk by the girls' bathroom and keep opening the door, pretending to throw each other in.

We have an assembly this afternoon for Remembrance Day. Some of us have to read the essays we wrote. My Grampie was in World War Two. I wrote about him and my Grammie's brother George. He died in the war. He was only eighteen. Grammie still cries almost every time she says his name. Mrs. M. asked us this morning if we were going to the Remembrance Day service at the Legion on Monday.

Mrs. M. told us a funny story about her youngest son. When he was about five, they were on their way to the Legion for the service and he asked her if today was the hot dog day, the cake day, or the hot chocolate day. She didn't understand what he meant at first then realized that they go to the Legion on Canada Day (the cake), for the older kids' baseball banquets (the hot dogs), and for Remembrance Day (hot chocolate). That's funny, because that's how Mom always gets Corey to come to Remembrance Day services. She bribes him away from the TV with the promise of hot chocolate.

November 12

Even the hot chocolate wasn't enough to get Corey out of bed yesterday morning. Mom stayed home with him and Dad took me to the Legion. We picked Grammie up on the way. She asked me to lay the wreath in memory of George. His last name was Wetmore, which I would normally find funny, but when they read his name I started to cry. I kept my head down and walked through the crowd as quickly as I could.

I asked Grammie yesterday about her Mom. I asked her how she was when George died. It sounded dumb when I said the words, "How was she?" I meant how was she? How did she act? Did she cry? Did she talk about him? Did she have pictures of him around? My Grammie's mother's name was Anne. That is where I got my middle name, that and the fact that my Mom is the biggest *Anne of Green Gables* fan ever born.

Grammie said, "You never get over the death of a child." George was the youngest and the only boy in a family of five. She told me that her Mom got a letter from George the day after they had gotten word that he had been killed in France. She waited five years before she opened it. She carried it everywhere she went and never talked about the letter until the day she opened it. She sat at her kitchen table and read the letter out loud to her husband and Grammie. She read it on the date George died, October 18th, five years later. She read it without emotion then walked across the room, lifted the lid on the wood stove, and dropped the letter in.

Anne never said his name again. Grammie said that a framed picture of him in his army uniform hung in the dining room. His clothes and all his things stayed in the little room at the top of the stairs, just the way he had left them until the house was to be sold after both of Grammie's parents died. The family always remembered George's birthday, a nephew was named after him, and the sisters always put flowers on his grave every October 18th, but Anne never said his name.

November 13

Something is wrong with Corey. Mom and Dad took him to Halifax this morning. Dad and Corey were in the car waiting to leave, but Mom stood at the bus stop with me. They don't know how long they are going to be gone. Mom kept hugging me and crying.

I do not want to be at school today. I just want to go home and cry. I want to go to my room, lie on my bed, pull my blankets up over my head, and bawl my frigging head off. Mom said I had to go to school. Grammie is picking me up at 3:00. Mom gave me money for the cafeteria. She signed my agenda and wrote Mrs. M. a note. She told me that there was nothing to worry about. Right! That's why she couldn't stop crying. That's why Dad got all choked up when he said goodbye to me. And I heard him say that word again last night.

Bradley Chalkers is the main character in *There's a Boy*.... He is a really weird kid with a lot of problems. He has a collection of little animals. The main ones are Ronnie and Bartholomew. Bartholomew is a brown and white ceramic bear. Ronnie is a little red rabbit. I don't know what she is made out of. The part Mrs. M. read this morning was really funny. It was sad, too, though, and I felt sorry for Bradley. Bradley was very upset and

Ronnie told him not to cry. I wish I had a small red rabbit that I pretended could talk to me. She would say, "Don't worry, Taylor. Corey will be fine. Your Mom and Dad will be home soon and everything will be OK. Don't be crazy, Taylor. Your brother does not have cancer!"

November 18

Grammie is not telling me anything. All she says is that it might take a lot of time for the doctors to do all the tests they need to do. She took me home for a few minutes yesterday so that I could pack more stuff. She said she didn't know how long I would be at her house so I should pack lots of clothes, just in case. I looked through my room and tried to pack everything I might need and some of my most important possessions. I looked at the china dog that Aunt Rachel gave me for Christmas last year. I like him OK but I've never really paid much attention to him. I put him in a sock and placed him in the outside pouch of my backpack. I decided I would call him Erno. I grabbed a stuffed turtle, too, so that Erno would have someone to talk to. The turtle's new name is Bartholomew.

We played dominoes. Grammie seemed really glad when I asked her to play. She won the first game and I won the next two. She was eleven years old when George was born. He was so small that they put him in an apple basket to sleep. They put the apple basket close to the wood stove to keep him warm.

George loved to play tricks on her. One time he put a huge bullfrog in her bed and hid, waiting to hear her scream. He was laughing hysterically as she pulled back the covers. The frog jumped from her bed and plopped into a basin of water on her bed stand. She hollered at George to catch it. He scrambled out from underneath the bed, knocked over the bed stand, and sent the basin crashing to the floor. The water spilled all over, the basin smashed to pieces, and the frightened frog landed on Grammie's foot. Her terrified screams brought their mother into the room and both Grammie and George got in big trouble.

November 20

Mom called last night. She reminded Grammie that I have a dentist appointment after school today. She talked to Grammie for quite a long time, but she didn't have much to say to me. She said everyone was OK and that she thought they would be home on the weekend. Dad was somewhere with Corey so I didn't get to talk to them. I can't believe how much I miss Corey. I cried when I got off the phone. I went into the bathroom so Grammie would not know.

Mrs. M. has been crying. I can tell by the look on her face. Her eyes are puffy and there are red blotches on her cheeks. When we got back from French class, she was sitting at her desk. Mrs. Shannon was sitting on the top of Luke's desk them moved. Luke stood beside his desk and it seemed like a long time before they noticed. Mrs. Shannon got off the desk and went over beside Mrs. M., leaned down, and hugged her. Some kids got out their journals and started to write. I just sat there in a bit of a daze thinking about how I much I would like to get a hug from my Mom.

I really hate going to the dentist. I hate sitting there with my mouth stuck wide open. I hate the feel of those slimy rubber gloves the girl wears. I hate her digging at my teeth. Corey gets to miss it, but I guess I would rather be me going to the dentist, than be him in a hospital having all kinds of needles and stuff.

November 21

I had no cavities. I got a new orange toothbrush and cherry- flavoured floss. I got a new tooth-brush for Corey, too. I also got him a bag of Snickers bars at the Co-op. Grammie said she would pay for them, but I wanted to use my own money.

Mrs. M. read for a long time this morning. Bradley ripped up his homework. He was so proud of having his homework done, but just before he passed it in, he ripped it up and threw it in the garbage. He wants to write a book report on the book that Carla is reading to him. Carla is the guidance counsellor and Bradley goes to see her almost every day. Things have been getting better for him since he started talking to Carla. Bradley really likes the book. If he does do the book report, he really hopes that he doesn't rip it up.

We have to write a book report. It is due on December 17. I am going to read *Anne of Green Gables*. That is not the kind of book I normally like to read, really. I want to read it because it is my Mom's favourite book. She has read it about a hundred times. I am going to read the copy she read when she was my age. It is in the bookshelf in the upstairs hall at Grammie's. Even if it is the most boring book in the world, I am going to make myself read it.

November 22

The first sentence in the book *Anne of Green Gables* is the longest beginning sentence I have ever read. It has 148 words in it, 149 if "well-conducted" is two words. It has three commas in it. There are two of these punctuation marks: "—." There were at least five words I had to look up in the dictionary. "Ferret" is a European polecat and it also means to drive out of hiding. ("She had ferreted out the whys and wherefores thereof.")

Right away I thought this book was going to be more than I could handle. I read the first sentence again and thought about my Mom reading it when she was my age. I kept reading after I counted the words and used the dictionary for a while. I kind of like the language of it and the old-fashioned way it sounds. But I am going to have to keep the dictionary on hand, I think.

List of ten words to look up in the chapter "Mrs. Rachel Lynde Is Surprised"

1. traversed
2. decorum
3. gauntlet
4. myriad
5. betokened
6. embowered
7. patriarchal
8. proverbial

9. qualms
10. ejaculated (I looked that up and it is definitely
   meaning number 2)

They are coming home today. I am trying not
to think too much about it. Grammie said to go
home on the bus and that she would be there. She
doesn't know what time they will get home. I am
going to help her make a welcome home supper.

November 25

I don't know how to write about this. All weekend I wanted Monday morning to come so I could
get to school. I wanted to be here doing school
stuff that would seem normal. All the normal
school stuff, but I forgot about journal. Just write.
Just write about whatever you are thinking. But
I am trying not to think. I can't write about what
I'm not thinking. But that's the thing, I can't think
about anything else. Holly is wearing a yellow
shirt. The Grade Fives just walked by on their
way to French class. I can hear Mr. McKay calling out spelling words next door. How can I write
down on paper what I am really thinking? I can't
write it and I can't talk about it. Who would I talk
to? Could I stand up and read? "They think my
brother might have cancer." Maybe I could write a

play for Erno and Bartholomew. I could hold them up behind a cardboard box with curtains and they could talk about it.

Erno: Have you ever heard the word "neuroblastoma"?
Bartholomew: No.

That was dumb. I don't want to do that. I don't want anyone to know. I don't want to know. I don't want to know half of what Mom and Dad told me. I don't want to think about this. I don't know what to do.

Mrs. M. says that you use a ; (it's called a semi-colon) something like you use a period to separate word groupings. It separates them but keeps them together so you can use a semi-colon to keep two thoughts together. She said I probably won't use semi-colons very often, but I can try to use them if I want to.

November 26

Mom is coming after school today to talk to Mrs. Montague, Miss Elliot, Mr. Caines, and Mr. Shea. She wants them to know. She says Corey will be missing a lot of school, and they have to know what is going on. She says they have to know about what our family is going through. Last night I told her I didn't want anyone to know. I knew I was being really selfish and I could hear myself screaming at her not to tell anybody, but I couldn't stop myself. I didn't want them to feel sorry for me. I didn't want them to ask me questions. I didn't want anyone to know! She tried to talk to me but I ran out of the kitchen towards my room. Corey was standing in the hall. He was just standing there, looking so silly in his Power Ranger jammies. So silly and so scared. All of a sudden it hit me. It wasn't just about me. This wasn't just happening to me. This was happening to Corey. It was his body that had hidden a tumour the size of a tennis ball. He was the one who had to lie on a table and let doctors stick long needles in him. He is the one who doesn't know what they are going to do to him next. I sat right down on the floor and cried. Corey sat down beside me and put his head on my shoulder. I could feel the top of his bristly buzz cut head on my cheek. Mom sat down beside us and we just sat there for a long time. She said we would go through this as a family. I told her that I was sorry for screaming at her, and then Corey and I both went to bed.

November 27

   Mrs. M. talked to me during French class. She asked me to stay behind and help her pass out some books. I knew what was coming. Mom said that Mrs. M. had hugged her yesterday. I really hoped that she wouldn't hug me. I knew that if she did I would lose it. She didn't. She just talked and told me she would do whatever she could to help me. Her eyes filled up when she said, "It's amazing what we can do when we have to." She told me not to be afraid to feel whatever I was feeling. She said, "You will have all kinds of feelings and none of them are wrong; they are just how you feel and you have to find a way through them." I really wanted to tell her some stuff but I couldn't open my mouth. I just stood there like a dummy. "It helps me to write about things," was the last thing she said. I thought about that as I hurried to the French room.

The books we passed out were called The *Summer of the Monkeys*. We are going to read the book together and do a writing project on it. We are going to condense each chapter and write it in picture book form. We will type the pages on the computer, then illustrate them. I am going to practise drawing monkeys because there will probably be monkeys on just about every page.

Mrs. M. finished *There's a Boy in the Girls' Bathroom* this morning. The book is in December's book order. I am going to buy it so that I have my own copy. It has just become one of my favourite books.

November 28

I started a journal at home. I am not going to let anyone see it. I am going to write whatever I am feeling. I am going to write things that I might want to say but that I never would. I haven't decided if I will write swear words in it if I am thinking a swear word. I can draw pictures in it and I can write pretend letters to people. I might write down my dreams if I remember them. I can write anything because no one will see it. If I look back and what I wrote was dumb, it won't matter. No one will see it. I am going to lock it in the cedar box that Dad brought me back last year from Boston. I will wear the key on a string. If I ever want to destroy my home journal, I will set fire to it in the outside fireplace.

November 29

Mrs. M. went home yesterday. She seemed fine all morning, but she didn't come back in the afternoon. I know she hadn't planned on leaving because she said we were going to the computer lab in the afternoon. We worked all writing class on our Chapter One write-ups, and she had marked everybody's rough copies and assigned us our computer partners. We had already written our homework in our agendas because she said we would be in the lab all afternoon. Mrs. M. always meets us at the downstairs door when we come in from the playground. If she isn't there for some reason then Mrs. Ashe is usually there to bring the line up. When no one was there we stood for quite a while waiting, then Thomas and Nick started up the stairs. We all followed them. Even after everyone was in the classroom, there was still no teacher. Mr. McKay looked in and told us to sit down and be quiet. He told us to get a book out or something. We did and the room quieted down to regular talking. Justin and Nick were fighting over the big atlas and I told them to shut up. After a few minutes Mrs. Ellen came in to the classroom. No one knew why she was in our room. She lined us up and told us that we were going to help her in the kindergarten this afternoon.

We packed our book bags and got our outdoor stuff. We were even going to go out for last recess with the little kids at the end of the day. Everyone forgot about going to the computer lab and the room was crazy with "free afternoon in the kindergarten" excitement. No one seemed to be too worried about Mrs. M. No one even asked

Mrs. Ellen where Mrs. M. was. A few minutes later when Mrs. Ellen sent Holly and me upstairs to get Holly's Epi-pen we saw Mrs. M. leaving the staff room. She had her coat on and Mrs. Shannon was walking beside her. She didn't even seem to see us. She is not here today, and I can still see her walking slowly through the hall. She looked so scared.

December

December 2

Corey is in the hospital for a few days. Mom is staying in with him, but Dad will be home at night. He is going to bring chicken home for supper tonight.

Mrs. M. is only going to work three days a week. She talked to us today and told us that she will be here on Mondays, Tuesdays, and Wednesdays until Christmas. She talked very slowly and I knew she was trying hard not to cry. She said that when she came back to school in September, she had been determined to do her best every day. She said that she had had to go home a couple of days and that she had had some days when she wasn't able to come to school. She said that we all had been so much help to her so far this year and she wants to be OK and be here teaching us every day. But, she said, right now she was having a hard time and that she needed to take care of herself and be strong for the month of December. She was crying by then. She said Zac's birthday was on December 5. She said Christmas was coming, and she knew that the first Christmas without Zac would be very difficult. She said that she hoped staying home two days a week would help her to be able to get through the times ahead. Nick asked her who our teacher would be. She told us that Mrs. Scott would come in on Thursdays and Fridays. She said she expected us to cooperate with Mrs. Scott and to keep working hard until Christmastime. After Christmas she plans to come back for the whole week again.

December 3

When Mom called last night I told her that I was on page 158 of *Anne of Green Gables*. Anne got Diana drunk. She thought she was giving her raspberry cordial but it was Marilla's currant wine. Raspberry cordial. I like the sound of that. "Cordial" means friendly, heartfelt, and sincere. Anne was just trying to be friendly. Mrs. Barry said that Anne was not a fit little girl for Diana to associate with. I can't believe how much I love this book.

Mom said that they took a piece of the tumour and sent it away. Corey is doing OK, and that they can come home tomorrow. Dad and I are going to clean the house tonight. I am going to set up all Corey's toys in the family room so that he will see them when he walks in. Grammie is going to send over her homemade macaroni and cheese and biscuits for our supper. Mom says that is her "comfort food."

We had a really long writing class this morning. Mrs. M. says that Mrs. Scott can do extra math on Thursdays and Fridays. We won't have writing class with Mrs. Scott so we will have longer writing classes during the first part of the week. I am really glad about that because I write better when Mrs. M. helps me. She always seems so excited about my writing and even when she gets me to fix things, I feel good about it. She told me today that Lucy Maud Montgomery had the manuscript of *Anne of Green Gables* rejected a lot of times before it was published.

December 5

Mrs. Scott is giving us some journal time. I think she was tired of telling Thomas and Nick to be quiet during science class and she needed a little break. She said she didn't care if we drew in our journals. I know Mrs. M. would care.

Today Zachary would have been twenty-one years old. I wonder what Mrs. M. is doing right now. Mom always goes through the same thing on our birthdays. She starts with, "This time (however many) years ago...." She tells us all about the trip to the hospital. She mentions how long it took for us to be born. She tells us what time we were born and how much we weighed. She tears up and tells us how wrinkled we were and all about our fingers and toes. I wonder if Mrs. M. is saying to herself, "This time twenty-one years ago...."

Mom always makes us a confetti cake with boiled icing for our birthdays. We always get a toy and an outfit. Grammie always comes over and Aunt Rachel always sends us a card with the amount of money in it that is our age. Zachary would be getting twenty-one dollars. Mrs. M. told her kids that she would pay them five hundred dollars when they turned nineteen if they didn't smoke. Zachary didn't smoke and he got his five hundred dollars on his nineteenth birthday. Just before his twentieth birthday he told his Mom that he thought he should get fifty dollars maintenance money for still not smoking. She told him she would pay it until he was twenty-one. He didn't get his twenty-one-year-old not- smoking money. Mrs. M. said that she was very proud of Zac for not smoking. A lot of his friends smoked, but he never did.

I will never smoke. It is gross. Uncle Paul smokes. I am going to ask Mom if Corey and I can get five hundred dollars when we turn nineteen, if we don't smoke.

December 9

Mrs. M. is reading us the book *The Best Christmas Pageant Ever*. The kids in the Herdman family are really mean and nasty. There is a Herdman in every grade. At our school we have the Lockhart family. They are pretty scary, too. Thank goodness there isn't one in Grade Four, but Corey has to put up with Peter Lockhart in his class because Peter failed last year. The Lockharts go on Victoria's bus and they get kicked off the bus all the time. Even the youngest one swears and pushes the other kids around.

I have the first eight pages of my *Summer of the Monkeys* picture book typed on the computer and illustrated. My monkeys looked like really bad gingerbread men at first, but I am getting better at drawing them.

December 11

We had a storm day yesterday. It was wonderful. I love it when Mom comes in and tells me I can go back to sleep. I hardly ever do but it is nice to just lie in bed knowing you don't have to get up. There was a lot of snow in our yard and I helped Dad shovel when he got home from work. I read most of the day. I finished reading *Anne of Green Gables* and started my book report. The last line in the book said, "God is in his heaven, all's right with the world." I wrote that line down in my home journal. Then I made a list of all the things I knew were not right with the world. I knew I could never write that list in this journal because I would cry my head off while I was writing it. I was right. I did cry my head off as the list got longer. I stopped when I wrote "#27: Kids needing oncologists."

   I know what oncologist means because I asked Mom after I heard her say it to Aunt Rachel on the phone last night. Mom and Dad have to go meet with someone named Dr. Saunders today. She is a child oncologist.

Ten things that are right with the world:

1. good books
2. storm days
3. good food to eat
4. good friends
5. a loving family
6. grandmothers

7. schools and good teachers
8. hospitals that can help people
9. snow to play in
10. good news

December 16

It was not good news. Mom called Mrs. M. on the weekend so she would know and I wouldn't be the one to have to tell her. How would I have told her? You don't just go up to people and say my brother has cancer, like you say my brother has a red shirt. Because if your brother has a red shirt, people don't look at you funny. They don't ask you questions that you don't understand the answers to. Yes, he has to have an operation. They are going to cut him open. They are going to try to take the tumour out. Mom says that they are going to treat it with radiation and chemotherapy. It doesn't sound like any kind of treat to me. Dad took Mom and Corey today to the hospital in Halifax for the operation. It is only eight days until Christmas, and my Mom and brother have gone to a hospital four hours away. Dad is coming right back to go to work the rest of the week and on Saturday he will take me to Aunt Rachel's to stay. Then Dad will go to Halifax, and if Corey can't come home for Christmas, Dad will come and get me and take me there to be with Mom, Corey, and him for Christmas Day.

I can't believe I am writing all this. I just want to get through this week. I will miss my own house and our Christmas stuff. Corey and I each get an ornament of our own on Christmas Eve. We pick a side of the tree and put all of our ornaments on that side and then sit there to open our presents. I have three Feliz Navidad ornaments. When I was little I thought the song "Feliz Navidad" said, "At least nothing died," and Mom and Dad thought that was hilarious. For three years they got me an ornament that said Feliz Navidad. It was funny at first but enough already. Last Christmas I told them not to buy me any more variations of Feliz Navidad ornaments.

We have a really nice nativity scene that we always put on the coffee table. Corey snapped the shepherd's staff off when he was little and now it looks like the shepherd is herding his sheep with a short stick. Grammie always comes on Christmas Eve and watches us open our ornaments and one present. On Christmas morning we open our stockings in Mom and Dad's bed. I always have to wake Corey up. Mrs. M. told us about a time that Zachary and Megan woke up their brother and told him it was Christmas morning. It wasn't, but he jumped out of bed all excited. They pulled that trick on him twice in one week before he stopped trusting them.

December 17

Dad took me Christmas shopping last night. I got everybody's presents. I got Mrs. M. a really nice teapot with a cup that sits on the top. It is in the shape of an apple. It says "#1 Teacher" on it. I will give it to her tomorrow because she won't be here Thursday or Friday. I wish I didn't have to come to school for the whole week. Mrs. M. and I both don't want Christmas to come this year. Everybody else seems so excited by it. I would like to just sleep through it. Then maybe when I woke up, everything would be normal.

I don't feel like writing anything today. I don't feel like thinking anymore about anything. Blah, blah, blah. That's what I think.

The Christmas Miracle of Jonathan Toomey. Mrs. M. finished reading us that book this morning. Pish posh. I like the sound of that. Pish posh! That is just how I feel.

December 18

I gave Mrs. M. her present. She really liked it. She said she was going to make a pot of tea in it every day over the Christmas holidays and think about me every time she poured the tea into her cup.

Holly gave Mrs. M. a gift certificate to a restaurant called the China Wok. Mrs. M. calls it her happy place. I don't know where my happy place is. I know where my happy place isn't, though. It isn't school for the next two days, when Mrs. M. isn't even going to be here. It isn't my house, with no Christmas decorations, when next door Mrs. Donaldson's house looks like a perfect Christmas fantasyland. It isn't Aunt Rachel's house at Christmas time. It isn't a hospital in a place called Halifax (should be called Hell-ifax).

January

January 7

I did not take my home journal with me over Christmas break. I left it locked in the box, and I hid the key in an old shoe in my closet. I packed only a few clothes, the presents for everybody, and Erno and Bartholomew. Aunt Rachel seemed really happy to see that I had Erno with me. I didn't tell her why I had brought him and how I hadn't paid any attention to him until I made him a crazy talking dog.

Corey is at school, too. Mom is driving him and picking him up all week so that he doesn't have to take the bus. I came with them this morning but I will probably go home on the bus.

Everybody has new clothes on. I am wearing a new shirt that Aunt Rachel gave me. I opened presents at her house before Dad came to get me. Mom gave me all the rest of the Anne books.

List of the Anne of Green Gables books:

1. Anne of Green Gables
2. Anne of Avonlea
3. Anne of the Island
4. Anne of Windy Poplars
5. Anne's House of Dreams
6. Anne of Ingleside

We ate Christmas dinner in the hospital cafeteria. They had Christmas napkins and little plastic wine glasses filled with red juice to make the families feel more festive. The dressing didn't look anything like Grammie's and there was no gravy. I barely ate a bite. Grammie is cooking us a turkey dinner this weekend. I am going to fill my plate with potatoes and dressing. I mash it all together and make it into a big mountain. Then I break up pieces of turkey on top and cover it all with gravy.

Corey starts his treatment next week. He can have the first part of it here, and then he will have to go back to Halifax, Mom thinks. I'm glad they get to stay here and I get to stay home. Grammie is planning to stay at our house next week, but she might have to go to Aunt Rachel's if she has the baby when she is supposed to. Her due date is January 15. That sounds funny to me, due date.

But that's all everyone has been talking about at our house, Aunt Rachel's due date. That and all the hospital stuff with Corey.

January 8

Mrs. M. started reading us *The Lion, the Witch and the Wardrobe* today. Grammie has a big wardrobe thing at her house and now I will always think of a magical land waiting beyond the coats whenever I open it. There are seven books in The Chronicles of Narnia. I am going to get them out of the public library and read them all.

We got our book reports back yesterday. Mrs. M. didn't give us a mark but wrote lots of comments on them. She told me she was a big fan of *Anne of Green Gables*, too.

After she passed our book reports out to us we had to go around and sign up four people who would agree to read the book that we wrote our book report on. Holly, Adrianna, and Kayla signed up right away, but I really had to work at finding a fourth person. Troy Kingston finally said he would. I thought that was pretty brave of him because all the other boys were teasing him, saying it was a girl's book. That really ticks me off. We read boy books, if there is such a thing. But they think they'll turn into girls if they read a girl book (if there is such a thing). In a month's time, if three of your four people have read your book, you get a book from Mrs. M.'s Free Book Box. I told Thomas I would read *Hatchet*. I told Holly I would read *The Miraculous Journey of Edward Tulane*. I told Troy I would read *Willow*. I told Adrianna I would read *A Handful of Time*. I have a lot of reading to do.

January 10

We just picked our writing goals for January today. We didn't have a writing goal for December because we were too busy with our *Summer of the Monkeys* projects. I am going to give my *Summer of the Monkeys* picture book to Aunt Rachel's new baby when he gets born. Obviously I would wait until he gets born, although he won't know he has the book then, any more than he would know it now. I will read it to him when he is old enough to listen. I keep saying he. They don't know what the baby is but everybody keeps saying he, not she or it. Aunt Rachel says if it is a boy they are going to call him Zachary. That is just a coincidence. I did not tell Aunt Rachel that that was my teacher's son's name. I didn't want her to know she was naming her son the same name as my teacher's son who died. And I didn't tell Mrs. M. that my aunt was going to name her baby the same name as the son she has no more. I guess if it is a boy and they do name him Zachary, I will have to tell Mrs. M. because she will ask me what his name is. She knows my Aunt Rachel is pregnant and having her baby in a few days. Maybe it will be a girl. The girl's name they have picked out is Madeline.

My writing goal for this month is voice. Mrs. M. says this is the hardest writing trait to teach. She says we know voice when we hear it in writing. She read us some passages out of books written by some of the authors we know quite well, like E. B. White, Roald Dahl, Louis Sachar, and Judith Blume. We guessed them all. She said that means that we hear voice in writing. She said that we have to let our own voice come through in our writing. Next, she read some of our writing to see if we could identify who had written it. She started with one of my stories and asked the class if they knew whose story it was. At first, when she started reading it, I felt really embarrassed. But she read it just the way she had read the other passages, as if it was good writing, interesting, and worth reading. Even though I could feel that my face was really red it was nice to hear her read my writing like that. A lot of my friends would know it was my piece of writing, and I figured they would call out whose story it was just from hearing the title, but it was Justin who guessed it was mine and he wouldn't have known it from the title. He wouldn't have known from my red face either, because he was sitting in front of me. He said he knew it was mine because it sounded like me. That made me feel really good. I am going to start a new piece of writing and work really hard at letting the voice of Taylor Anne Broderson come through loud and clear.

January 13

Liam Caines had my copy of *The Lion, the Witch and the Wardrobe* when he was in Mrs. M.'s class in Grade Four. His name is written inside the front cover. There are six other kids' names including mine. Liam Caines is the principal's son. He goes to school in Manitoba now, at the Winnipeg School of Ballet. I think that is really neat. I wonder if he will get famous.

Ten things I would like to be famous for:

1. writing a book that gets on Amazon.com
2. collecting the most Archie books
3. setting a world record in Sudoku
4. writing a series that gets more popular than Harry Potter

5. *setting a world record for the most books read in one year*
6. *winning Canadian Idol*
7. *owning the most books in the world*
8. *writing my biography*
9. *having a movie made from one of my books like they did with Louis Sachar's book Holes*
10. *curing cancer*

Curing cancer should have been my #1 thing. I know that it would be more important than any of the other things I put down. I also know that curing cancer is not something I could ever do, but I hope somebody else does, and I hope they hurry up.

January 14

Aunt Rachel went into the hospital early this morning and I don't know if she has had the baby yet. Grammie said if the baby is born today, she will take the bus to Aunt Rachel's tomorrow and stay with her for a few days.

I read *The Miraculous Journey of Edward Tulane* last night. I read it all in one night because the print is quite big and there were pictures. The pictures are really nice. I read Holly's hardcover copy that her Aunt Susan gave her for her birthday. I love holding a hardcover book. Holly was happy that she could check me off this morning. I was her third person so she will get her free book. I don't know whether I will get mine or not. It takes a lot of time and some dedication to read *Anne of Green Gables*, and I don't know if my people have what it takes. I haven't even asked because I don't want to know if they haven't started. I am almost done reading *Hatchet*. I have been trying to read The Magician's Nephew at the same time. I can only do so much.

January 15

Aunt Rachel had a boy. His name is Zachary Richard Collingwood. Grammie told me how much he weighed, but I don't remember what she said. She said it like it was a really good thing with her eyebrows raised a bit and talked about Aunt Rachel like she had just got the winning goal in a soccer game or something. I told Mrs. M. about the baby as soon as I saw her this morning. I thought it would be the best thing to just get it over with and not to wait until she asked me. She seemed OK when I said what the baby's name was and there were so many other kids telling her stuff she didn't have time to say anything except, "Isn't that nice."

Mrs. M. just finished reading us the chapter from *The Lion, the Witch and the Wardrobe* called "A Day with the Beavers." I loved the picture of Mr. and Mrs. Beaver's den. It looked really cozy. Two bunk beds were built into the side of the walls. A woodstove was against the other wall and overhead there were hams, onions, and kitchen utensils hanging from the ceiling. Mrs. Beaver's sewing machine and rocking chair were at the front of the picture. I tried really hard to listen to the chapter when Mrs. M. was reading but as soon as she read the title it made me think about Corey.

Corey is a beaver expert. He loves beavers and knows everything there is to know about them. Last year some beavers built a lodge in our pond. He watched them every day and became obsessed with beaver information. He has beaver books all over his room. He has a beaver bedspread, four beaver posters, a collage of beaver pictures he cut out of his Owl magazines, a huge beaver calendar, many stuffed beavers, and about twenty chewed beaver sticks of all lengths and sizes. Mom won't let him put any more sticks in his room. Dad told him to leave some wood for the beavers.

I'm going to take my copy of The Lion, the Witch and the Wardrobe in to show Corey that beaver chapter. I know real beavers don't have homes

like that but I think he would like to see it anyway.
I am going to take him in a couple of his stuffed
beavers, too.

January 16

Mrs. M. read from her journal yesterday. The
whole entry was about the name Zachary. She
started by writing about my aunt calling her new
baby Zachary. She said that when she named her
baby Zachary it was a very uncommon name.
She had heard of the name from the singer John
Denver. His son's name was Zachary. She liked it
right away and put it on her long list of names
when she was expecting her first baby. Lots of
people had strong feelings about the name. They
thought it was awful. She said that in some ways
that made her more determined to name him
Zachary. In the first few years his name was still
not common and lots of people would say, "What
is his name?" as if it was the strangest name ever.
When Zac started school, he was the only one
in the school with that name and you still didn't
hear it very much, she said. Then, all of a sudden,
it was being used a lot. Right now, she said she
could think of at least five Zacharys in our school.
She wrote about the Zachary that is in Grade One
right now. He was named after her son because

the boy's dad was her Zac's counsellor at camp. He had taught Zac to paddle a canoe and he took him on several canoe trips. Zachary was fourteen when Mike, the camp counsellor, and his wife had a baby boy and called him Zachary. She said that she knew of one other person who had named their baby Zachary because of her Zachary. When Mrs. M. was in her last year of university learning how to be a teacher, Zachary was one-year-old. His babysitter had two kids, a girl and a boy. They loved Zachary and even after Mrs. M. moved, her family visited the babysitter's family whenever they could. When the babysitter's son grew up, he named his second little boy Zachary after Mrs. M.'s Zachary. She wrote that it made her very happy that there were two Zacharys because of her son and what he had meant to the dads of those two boys. She was crying quite a bit by the time she finished reading us that entry and quickly told us to put our journals away and get our snacks for recess. Holly told me I shouldn't feel guilty about telling her about Aunt Rachel's baby, because it seemed to her that it was happy and sad crying at the same time, if there is such a thing.

January 17

Dad and I went in to the hospital last night.

Corey looks so small in that big hospital bed. He is hooked up to some tubes that go to a bag of something on a stand. The stand has wheels and he has to take it with him if he gets up to go to the bathroom. Mom said that he has been too weak to get up for the bathroom so they have to put a silver bowl thing under him when he has to go. I walked down the hall to the playroom when the nurse came in to do something to Corey. She pulled the curtain across and Mom and Dad told me to step out of the room. Shrek was already partway through on the TV in the playroom and I just watched it for a little while.

Corey was really glad that I had brought him two of his stuffed beavers. He said that they were his favourite two.

I am going to stay the whole weekend at Holly's. Her Mom doesn't have to work this weekend. Mom called this morning and told Dad that Mrs. Jones said I could go there for the weekend. I packed really quickly so that I could go there from the bus. Dad said that Corey had had a very bad night. He was really sick. Mom wants Dad to come to the hospital after work. She is going to come home for a little while. She needs to have a shower and a little break, Dad said. Dad told me that the tube that was hooked to Corey's arm was putting strong medicine in his body and that the medicine was making him very sick. I wanted to ask Dad why they would give him medicine that would make him sick but I had to hurry to my room to get my stuff packed.

I finished *Hatchet* in S.S.R. Brian got rescued. It must have been very weird to be alone in the wilderness all that time. He had a hatchet with him when the plane crashed. I thought that they didn't let you take stuff like that on planes.

I usually like going to Holly's, but I don't really want to go today. I wish I could just go home and be there when Mom comes home. I wish Corey was home and that everything was normal.

January 20

It is really cold out today. It said on the radio that with the wind chill it is -31 degrees Celsius. We didn't go out at recess.

We went to the hospital yesterday afternoon. Corey did not get out of bed. I read to him for a while but I don't know if he was really listening. He slept most of the time. Mom and Dad left us alone and went down to the cafeteria for coffee.

I had an OK time at Holly's. We watched a scary movie on Friday night but I didn't think it was scary at all. I thought it was just really stupid. On

Saturday we went to her Aunt Susan's. She has a rink in her yard and we skated all afternoon. We had stew for supper, but it didn't taste anything like Mom's stew. Holly's Mom didn't even make doughboys. I went to their church on Sunday morning and then Dad picked me up. All weekend I tried to get up enough nerve to ask Holly's Mom some questions about Corey and the hospital. I wanted to ask her about the medicine, but every time I tried to open my mouth I couldn't get any words out.

January 21

We are going snowshoeing this afternoon. We will walk up MacPherson's Hill and snowshoe on the roads that wind through their Christmas tree farm. Mrs. MacPherson is going to have hot chocolate ready for us when we come out of the woods. She always dresses up like Mrs. Claus when she is selling Christmas trees, but I don't imagine she will today. I am glad it is not as cold as it was yesterday.

I talked to Mom and Corey on the phone last night. He can probably come home by the weekend. They have given him all the medicine they can for now and he can come home now to get his strength back.

Aunt Rachel e-mailed us some pictures of baby Zachary. He looks like a little elf. Mom said that maybe we will go see the baby on our March break.

We have to copy our homework down before lunch today because Mrs. M. said we will probably just get back from snowshoeing at bus time. Victoria's, Thomas's, and Kayla's moms and Justin's dad are coming with us. I wish my mom was home. She would have come for sure because she is good friends with Mrs. MacPherson. I am allowed to call Mrs. MacPherson "Jane," but I won't today.

January 22

I spent a lot of time on my butt yesterday afternoon. I kept tripping on my snowshoes or stepping on one with the other one. Good thing that there was a lot of snow to soften my landing. By the end I just took the snowshoes off and walked on the tracks that the others had made.

I finished reading all the books that I signed up to read so now I can get back to the other books I want to read. I am going to read one Anne book, then one Narnia book, then one *Series of Unfortunate Events* book, and keep reading in that order until I get through all three series.

Adrianna and Troy have finished reading *Anne of*

Green Gables. There is some hope. The other two people have fifteen days to finish.

January 23

We are all writing quietly in our journals. It almost felt trance-like as we walked back to our desks a few minutes ago, after Read Aloud. We have been crying. Most of us have been anyway.

When Mrs. M. reads to us during Read Aloud she sits on the couch. Every day she invites four kids to sit on the couch with her: she's in the middle and two kids are on each side. The rest of the class sits on the floor in front of the couch. Today I was sitting on the couch beside her and Maggie was beside me. Mrs. M. was reading the chapter called "Deeper Magic from Before the Dawn of Time." The White Witch and her evil army had just killed Aslan. Susan and Lucy were hidden in the bushes and had seen it all. Mrs. M. started reading the paragraph at the bottom of page 173. We had our novels and most of us were following along as she read. The paragraph started like this: "I hope no one who reads this book has been quite as miserable as Susan and Lucy were that night; but if you have been—if you've been up all night and cried till you have no more tears left in you..."

Mrs. M. couldn't continue. She sat with her head

down and made small gasping noises. Tears were streaming down her cheeks. I was right beside her and could feel her shaking. She held the book close to her like you would hold a small kitten. Maggie was crying beside me, and I could tell other kids were crying, too, even though I didn't really look at any one. After what seemed like a long time, Mrs. M. read the rest of the paragraph: "You will know that there comes in the end a sort of quietness. You feel as if nothing was ever going to happen again."

Mrs. M. closed the book and put it down on the floor in front of her. She began telling us about the night that Zac died. They had gotten the call at 3:00 in the morning and they didn't know he was dead; they only knew he had been in an accident. Mrs. M. and her husband drove toward where the accident had happened to meet and follow the ambulance to the hospital. The whole way Mrs. M. said that she had prayed that Zac was all right. They stopped and waited at the ferry. Her sister-in-law met them there, and they got into her car, came across on the ferry, and waited for the ambulance to come. After a few minutes an RCMP car pulled up to escort them to the hospital. The officer stepped up to the car and Mrs. M.'s husband got out. He walked with the officer and leaned into the police car to talk to his brother, who was on the phone from the site of the accident. Mrs. M. told us that when her husband straightened back up outside the car, she knew that Zachary was dead. At that moment she told us that she cried a cry that was like nothing she had ever known and she felt like it would never end, and like the book said, she felt like nothing would ever happen again because this was the end.

Mrs. M. stopped talking and looked slowly around at us all. Holly quietly started to talk about the day her grandmother died and what it had been like when her Mom told her that her Grammie had fallen down the stairs and that she was dead. Chelsea Dobbin put her hand up, and Mrs. M. nodded at her, and Chelsea told the class that her Mom had had a baby girl who died when she was just fourteen hours old. Chelsea had been in the hospital with her Mom and Dad and held the baby even after she stopped breathing and the family had cried for a long time before the nurse took the baby away. Nick said he had cried when they had to have his dog Kramer put to sleep. A lot of other kids told about things that had happened in their families. I was talking before I even realized it and when the words came out, I couldn't believe I had told the whole class how afraid I was that Corey was going to die. Mrs. M. put her arm around me, and I let the tears fall as someone else told about losing a person they loved.

Mrs. M. stood up after a while and said, "Don't we all look a fright? If someone came in right now, they would wonder what in the world I was doing to you. Let's pull it together and write in our journals for a while and I think we all deserve a few extra minutes of recess."

Mrs. M. said she would meet us outside after recess and give us extra time. She said we could go on the primary playground, which for some unknown reason is a big treat after you get too big for that playground.

January 24

I get to stay home all weekend. I am going to clean my room and organize my bookshelf. I am going to put all my books in alphabetical order. I am going to take all my little kid books and put them in Corey's room. There are a few I will keep in my room that are really special to me. Corey wouldn't want my Jillian Jiggs books anyway. The Franklin books belong to both of us, but I will put them in Corey's room for him to read.

I think Mom and Corey will be home when I get home. Dad is taking this afternoon off work and picking them up. Last night we put Mom and Dad's bedroom TV and DVD player in Corey's room. Dad said that Corey will probably be in bed most of the time for a few days anyway.

We did laundry last night, too. Dad put everything in all together and I know Mom wouldn't have been happy about that, but we dried all the clothes, folded them, and put everything away so she will never know. She won't know that we didn't do the dishes every night either. We used paper plates for the first few days until they ran out. We did load the dishwasher, but with just the two of us it didn't get full all week.

The roll call question on Friday is always, "What are your weekend plans?" When I answered today I said I wasn't sure what my weekend plans were. I did not want to tell anyone how excited I was to have a normal weekend at home with my family, my whole family.

My weekend plans:

1. tell Corey about Peter Lockhart getting kicked out of school this week
2. ask Mom to make stew
3. eat two doughboys

4. watch all the Saturday morning cartoons with Corey in his room
5. help Mom make Corey some peanut butter cookies
6. play Lego with Corey for as long as he wants to
7. play dominoes with the whole family and Grammie
8. write in my home journal
9. clean my room like I already said

January 28

I was late for school yesterday morning. The class had already written in their journals when I arrived. We all overslept. Dad and I rushed around and got ready as fast as we could. Mom and Corey stayed in bed. I just had Honeynut Cheerios for breakfast. Dad gave me money for the cafeteria.

Mrs. M. came out in the hall to talk to me while I was at my locker. She asked me how everyone was doing. She told me I could talk to her anytime. Mrs. M. gave me a box of school books and stuff that Miss Elliot had sent over for me to take home to Corey. There was a Get Well card on the top of the box that the kids in his class had made him. I stared at a big picture that somebody had drawn and coloured on the card. The brown marker they had used was running out and part of what I think was supposed to be a beaver looked barely coloured at all. Someone had printed "Get Will

Corey." That is not a good thing to tell a sick kid.

Corey has no hair. It has all fallen out, even his eyebrows. When he had his school pictures taken he hadn't had his hair buzzed yet, and he looks so different in that picture compared to how he looks now. Mom says that after his treatments his hair will grow back. He has to have more treatments. He will be home for three weeks, and then he has to go to Halifax again. He will have more chemotherapy there and they will give him radiation at the same time. That is what the medicine in his tube was, chemotherapy medicine. The medicine made his hair fall out because it is really powerful. Mom says it has to be powerful to kill the cancer cells that are in his body. He is eating hardly anything. Mom gave him a can of really thick liquid last night. It smelled like chocolate. Corey didn't want to eat it or drink it; I guess it looked way too thick to drink.

Mrs. M. finished reading *The Lion, the Witch and the Wardrobe* this morning. We have to do a project on it. It is due on February 15.

January 29

That thick chocolate-smelling stuff Corey has to swallow is called Pedia Sure. There are strawberry and vanilla flavours, too, but I don't think they taste any better, judging from Corey's reaction. I read the ingredients on the case. Each can has twenty-two ingredients in it, thirteen of them listed as nutrients and thirteen listed as vitamins. That makes a total of forty-eight things in one can of thick gunk that Corey has to drink four times a day.

Aunt Rachel is bringing the baby and coming to visit next week. I don't know why I wrote that she is bringing the baby. Of course she is bringing the baby. Mom talked to her on the phone for a long time last night. I could hear them talking when I was lying in bed trying to go to sleep. I couldn't hear what Mom was saying. Her voice just sounded like a hum. But at one point I could tell that she was crying. I really wanted to go into her room and do something, like hug her, pat her back, or just sit close beside her. I didn't, though. Instead I got up, got my home journal out of its hiding place, and wrote a whole lot of stuff. I didn't even read what I had written after I finished. I got into bed, hugged the journal to my chest, and cried. I almost fell asleep that way but caught myself and jumped up and locked the journal away. If I fell asleep with it, Mom or Dad might have found it when they checked on me before they went to bed. I know they check on me every night because sometimes I just pretend to be asleep. Sometimes it's just Mom or just Dad and sometimes it is both of them. They always tuck my blankets up around my neck, even in the summertime. They always kiss my cheek. That is a hard thing not to react to when I am awake because it tickles. "Goodnight, Dolly Girl. I love you," my Mom always says. "Goodnight, Toad. I love you," my Dad always says. I don't know why Dad calls me Toad but he always has. One time when Corey was little he saw a toad outside and said "Daddy, look at the little Taylor."

January 30

Corey ate some pudding last night. Grammie makes the best chocolate pudding known to mankind. She was at our house yesterday and made some for our supper. Everyone was so excited when Corey asked for a bowl of it and even more excited when he actually ate it, all of it.

I asked Victoria to come overnight tomorrow. I haven't asked Mom yet, but I'm sure she will let her come. I will call Victoria tonight and tell her what Mom says.

January 31

Mom said NO. I begged her but she said she was too tired. I don't get that at all. What does being too tired have to do with it? It's not like she has to look after us. We would have spent most of the time in my room, and Victoria doesn't expect my mother to wait on her. Mom's not too tired to have Aunt Rachel and a new, crying baby come to visit. I finally called Victoria to tell her that she wasn't allowed to come after I tried everything I could think of to convince Mom to change her mind.

February

February 3

  February is Black History Month. Mrs. M. is reading us a book called *Roll of Thunder, Hear My Cry*. Mom did not hear my cry last night. She is not hearing anything I say these days. The book is about the Logan family: Stacey, Cassie, Christopher John, and Little Man. Mrs. M. read us another book about them last year. It was called *Song of the Trees*.

  My February writing goal is "ideas." Most of the time when I am writing I am bursting with ideas. Bursting: teeming, overflowing, crawling, alive with, packed, jammed, like sardines in a can, overloaded, swollen, overstuffed, bloated.

February 5

  I got to hold Zachary last night. He was sound asleep and my arm got pins and needles because I held him for such a long time. Aunt Rachel asked me if I wanted to try changing him but I said, "Not a chance." Baby poop is really gross! Any poop is really gross, I guess. Corey held him for a little while, too, but Zachary was awake and cried the whole time Corey was holding him.

Kayla finished reading *Anne of Green Gables*. I'm going to pick a book that I think Corey will like. He must be so bored staying home every day. He can't even have a friend over because Mom is afraid that he might catch a cold or something.

February 6

I started my *The Lion, the Witch and the Wardrobe* project last night. Dad helped me. He cut the plywood for me. I am making a large wardrobe with doors that open. I am going to paint a scene showing Narnia on the piece of plywood at the back of the wardrobe. I started drawing the scene last night and hope to do some more on it tonight. We are going to Grammie's for supper so it depends how long we stay whether or not I will get to work on it. Corey has a bit more energy these days. He is eating a bit, too. Grammie asked him on the phone last night what he wanted her to make him. He said creamed corn. Gross! Aunt Rachel brought him a Toronto Blue Jays cap and he wears it 24/7.

Aunt Rachel is staying until Mom and Corey go to Halifax. Last night Mom and Dad came in just after I had gone to bed. They both sat down on the bed beside me, and I wondered what I had done wrong. They were there to talk about Halifax, they said. I really didn't want to talk about it. I had been trying hard not to think about the 18th of February. With Aunt Rachel and the baby here and Corey seeming to be better, I was trying to pretend that Halifax wouldn't happen. I don't want Mom to go away again. They told me that Dad would be going with them for the first week anyway. While Dad is gone Grammie will stay at our house so that I don't have to be away from home. I didn't say anything the whole time they were talking. I felt mad, but being mad is stupid because I know it isn't their fault. Part of me wanted to beg them to let me go to Halifax, too, so that at least I could be with them and not be home alone. I know I'm not going to be alone; Grammie will be here. I wanted to cry but I didn't. I lay there staring at the glow-in-the-dark stars and moons on my ceiling and said nothing. Dad was holding Mom's hand, and she kept patting my hair with her other hand. I could tell that she was trying hard not to cry, too. I felt scared. Scared for her and scared for Corey. I wanted to ask questions about radiation but I didn't. They both kissed me goodnight, and I just nodded my head and turned over toward the wall. They turned out the light and left my room. I lay there shaking, holding in my sobs so that they wouldn't hear them and come back in. I am going to try not to think about the day they leave and just concentrate on the days that we still have before they go. I know that writing about this is not not thinking about it, but from now on I am not going to think about it. Twelve days of not thinking about Halifax.

February 7

I painted the scene on the back of the wardrobe last night. I made the lamppost really big. Mrs. M. taught us about foreground and background in art class. The lamppost is in the foreground. Dad is going to help me glue the wardrobe pieces together tonight. We will use wood glue.

Most of us got to pick a book from Mrs. M.'s Free Book Box today. She gave bookmarks to the kids who didn't have their three people. First we had to meet with the people that read our book and discuss it. We talked about what we liked about the book. We had to write a short summary about the book, list the main characters, and write two questions we would like to ask the author. I think Mrs. M. made us do that so we would catch anyone who said they read the book but really didn't. It will take us a few days to meet in all of our groups. She gave us our free books even if we didn't have time to get all the groups done, so I guess she trusts us. I picked a non-fiction book to give to Corey. It is called The Scoop on Poop. He will think that is really funny.

We are all going to the movie theatre tonight. Grammie is going to come over and babysit Zachary. Mom said Corey could go even if there could be people there who might have a cold or something. She said it would be good for him to get out of the house.

February 11

We saw the movie The Rookie. It was about baseball and Corey really liked it. Uncle Richard came, too. He was at our house when I got home from school on Friday. He stayed for the whole weekend and drove home early this morning. He brought Corey a video game. I was a little disappointed that he didn't bring me anything, but I tried hard not to show it. I know I'm not the one who is sick.

It was fun to have so many people around all weekend. Holly came over for a while on Saturday, too. Mrs. Jones brought Corey some activity books.

Uncle Paul came to visit, too, and stayed over Saturday night. Dad, Uncle Richard, and Uncle Paul were making so much noise during Hockey Night in Canada that I couldn't get to sleep. I don't know how Corey and baby Zachary slept through it.

We had a big feast yesterday. Mom and Aunt Rachel cooked all day. Mom put some of the things that they made in the freezer. I love Aunt Rachel's homemade lasagna. I brought a piece today to heat up in the cafeteria microwave for my lunch.

February 12

We got the doors on the wardrobe. One is a bit higher than the other one, but you don't really notice when they are wide open, which is the way they will be to show the painting of Narnia. Mom and Aunt Rachel helped me make coats to hang in the wardrobe. They got some old coats at Frenchy's, and I cut a pattern out of newspaper and cut the material for smaller coats. One of them was even a fur coat. I bent some wire to make coat hangers that were the right size. I just have to finish sewing one coat and put buttons on them all.

February 14

Valentine's Day. We are passing out valentines at

recess time. I didn't put anyone's name on mine; I just signed them. They are all the same so that no one will think I gave a mushier one to "someone special." Believe me, there is no one special that I would give one to.

Mrs. M. showed us Robert Munsch's website in writing class today. The website was talking about Robert Munsch's book Love You Forever. Mom reads us that book all the time. The website said that Robert Munsch wrote it after he and his wife lost two babies. The rhyme in the book was a song that stuck in his head after the babies died. He said that he would cry every time he tried to sing it out loud. Then one time when he was telling stories to an audience in a big theatre, he began making up a story around the song. The story he made up became the book Love You Forever.

February 17

Dad drove me to school this morning so that I wouldn't have to bring the wardrobe on the bus. The classroom is filled with projects. We are going to present them this afternoon. Parents are invited to come in to see them. Mom is going to come. I am glad it is today that we are doing it because if it was tomorrow she wouldn't be here. It is just about time but it isn't yet so I don't need to think about her leaving. My wardrobe looks to be the biggest project. Mrs. M. put them all at the back of the room. We are not supposed to look at them until they are presented. Most of the projects are in garbage bags. Some kids didn't bring them in. Their parents are bringing them in when they come this afternoon.

February 18

Mom left a big box for me in the family room. She decorated the top of it with ribbons and bows. She wrote my name in huge letters on the sides of the box. There was a letter inside the box. The letter was a poem she made up about how much she would miss me. It was pretty corny, and she really pushed the rhyming thing. She is no better at writing poems than I am. Inside the box there were some wrapped presents. Each present has a tag with a date on it. I didn't count the presents but I know that there are more than seven. The poem told me that I could open a present every day until Mom and Corey get back home again. I didn't see the box until this morning. Grammie was there when I got up, and Mom, Dad, and Corey were already gone. I had planned to get up early enough to say goodbye, but when I heard them this morning, I pretended I was still asleep. I didn't want to see them go, so I let on to Grammie when she came to wake me that I hadn't heard them. I saw the box just as I was leaving for the bus so I only had time to read the letter and look in at the presents. I didn't open today's present. I am going to wait every day until I get home from school before I open the present.

Most of the projects were really neat. Thomas made a shield and sword. The shield has a crest with a painted lion on it. The tip of the sword was painted red to show blood left on from when Peter killed the wolf in the battle. Maggie made a papier maché sculpture of the White Witch. It was really good but I didn't tell her that. There were quite a few wardrobes but they all looked different. Mine was the biggest one. All of our projects are set up in the library. I hope nobody touches them or steals anything from them. Last year Holly lost some of her dollhouse furniture from a project she did that was on display in the library. She thought Miranda Lockhart stole them but she couldn't prove it.

February 19

Yesterday's present was a cross stitch kit to make a picture of Anne of Green Gables. Mom wrote a little note on a sticky paper inside that said she was so glad that I read her favourite book. She said I should start it while Grammie was there so she could help me if I needed help.

We are going to have our winter carnival next week. Every day is going to have a different theme. Monday is pyjama day. Tuesday is backwards day. Wednesday is crazy hat day. Thursday is sports day. Friday is crazy hair day, but our class won't be here because we are going to Mrs. Montague's house for our winter trip. She took us last year, too. It was really fun. We will walk a long way down a road through the woods across from her house. We will be on teams and her husband will show us how to gather wood and build a fire. We have to build our fire and make a can of snow melt. The first team to get their water to boil wins. Then we will cook hotdogs and marshmallows on our fires. After we eat we will walk back up to Mrs. M.'s house and go sliding. She has a really good hill in front of her house. Last year my team won. Thomas said we won because Kayla's Dad helped us. Thomas's team didn't even get their fire to go. It just kept smoking. So much for the saying, "Where there's smoke there's fire."

February 20

We started a health unit on the human eye yesterday. Mrs. M. got us to imagine what our lives would be like if we couldn't see. She blindfolded Thomas and asked him to get up to sharpen his pencil. We all laughed at him as he stumbled his way over toward the wall where the pencil sharpener is. Mrs. M. took off the blindfold and asked him what it was like to not have your eyes to help you. After that she passed out diagrams of the human eye that did not have the parts labeled. She put up a poster showing the parts of the eye. She said that she wanted us to look at the poster and label our diagrams. She pointed to the cornea. Then she showed us a gold medallion in a green velvet case. The front of the medallion said "A Gift of Life." She asked us what we knew about organ donation. Isaac said his uncle had had a liver transplant. Isaac often wears a tee shirt that says "Don't Take Your Organs to Heaven… Heaven Knows We Need Them Here." Becky said that her grandmother had given her Uncle Reggie a kidney. Mrs. M. told us that corneas can be donated also. She turned the medallion over and read what it said on the back: "In Recognition, Zachary Montague, April 2001." She went on to tell us that the week before Zac died, Megan had come home and told her about an assembly they had had at school that day. A woman had talked to

them about cornea transplants. Mrs. M. said that
the night Zac died, somehow in all the grief and
confusion that she was feeling this came to her
mind and she frantically asked her sister-in-law
to find out if there was anything of Zachary's that
could be donated. Zachary had died instantly, and
she thought it would be too late to use his organs
but she thought of his eyes. Someone ran out to
ask the Mountie if it was possible. She was told
that his corneas could be harvested and that the
officer was calling the hospital to inform them
of the family's request. That was the word she
said they used, "harvested." Shortly after that, the
phone rang. It was the eye bank and the person
calling asked Mrs. M's sister-in-law if the mother
was aware of what she was doing. Mrs. M. said she
remembered thinking that she was anything but
aware, but she calmly answered the questions so
that they could go ahead and use Zachary's corneas to help someone else. Afterwards Megan told
her Mom that she was worried that they might
not be able to use Zachary's corneas. She remembered at least two times that Zac had accidentally
gotten spray paint in his eyes. But they did use
them, Mrs. M. told us. She said that on the day
of Zachary's funeral the phone was ringing just
as they were ready to leave and that she almost

hadn't answered it. She did answer it, though, and the person on the phone told her that at that very moment Zachary's corneas were being given to two different people. Zachary was giving two people the gift of sight. By the time Mrs. M. got to that part she was crying really hard. Kayla who was sitting right beside where Mrs. M. was standing stood up and hugged Mrs. M. Any other time it would have seemed weird to see someone hug the teacher but I was really glad that Kayla did. Mrs. M. sat down on the couch and wiped her eyes as we all quietly started labeling the diagrams.

February 21

I almost opened my present this morning before I left for the bus. I didn't, though, because I like the anticipation of it during the day. On the weekend I think I will open the present after lunch. That way I'll have all morning to look forward to it. I counted the packages last night. Mom put twenty things in the box. I hope they are not away that many days. I wonder if they get home sooner than that if Mom will tell me to open all the presents that are left, or if she will put them away for the next time they have to go. I don't know if they will have to go to Halifax again. I don't know anything really. Wednesday's present was a Blue

Jays cap just like the one Aunt Rachel gave Corey.
I wore it until bedtime. I tucked all my hair up under the cap and looked in the mirror pretending
I had no hair. I could still see that I had eyelashes
and eyebrows, though, and Corey doesn't have his.
Some of the presents are big. When I picked them
up to count them I tried not to handle them or
shake them. I didn't want to guess what they are.

  The week went by quite quickly, a lot faster than
I thought it would. We are going to go to Grammie's tomorrow because she wants to water her
plants and do some baking at her own house.
I am going to help her make molasses cookies
and maybe some other things. I don't know if
we are sleeping at her house tomorrow night or
coming back to our house. Dad is coming home
Sunday. He should be home by lunchtime, Grammie thinks. I will wait until he gets home before I
open Sunday's present. Yesterday's present was
a bottle of No More Tears shampoo. I'm not sure
what that was all about, and there was no note
with it. I guess Mom is just reminding me to wash
my hair.

  I have been writing letters to Mom and Corey in
my home journal. I have been writing whatever I
think of, not writing like it was a letter that was
really being sent to them. I think I will write real

letters to them, though, if Dad thinks they will be there long enough to get them in the mail. I wrote a lot of questions in my "not sending letters" that I would not ask for real. I guess I could really ask Corey if his head was itchy when his hair was falling out. But he might not want to think about it. I definitely wouldn't ask him what it feels like to pee in that silver bowl thing. I wonder if it is really cold. I could ask him what the food is like, but I don't know if he is eating real food. Does he close his eyes when they give him radiation? Is it a bright light like an X-ray? I had to have my arm X-rayed when I fell off the monkey bars in Grade One. I chipped a bone. I didn't need a cast, though; I just had to have my arm in a sling for a few days. Does Mom sleep in the chair or do they give her a bed at nighttime? How does she wash her hair and take a shower? Does she put on pyjamas or sleep in her clothes? Does she get to watch Oprah? My real letter should probably just be about a few things that are happening here. "How are you? I am fine. Hope you are the same." Just dumb stuff like that that won't make her feel bad, be homesick, or worry about me. I don't think I can write letters like that, so I guess I won't write real letters to them.

February 24

Winter carnival week. I wore my snowflake pyjamas and my teddy bear housecoat. I feel pretty
stupid but almost everybody else looks just as
dumb. Thomas is wearing fire truck pyjamas. Nick
has on Scooby Doo pyjamas and a Teenage Ninja
Mutant Turtle housecoat. It is a little hard to take
a French teacher who is wearing a long flannel-
ette nightgown and moose slippers seriously. Mrs.
M. is wearing a red housecoat over blue pyjamas
with sheep on them.

Friday's present was the whole boxed set of the
Narnia series. I am very glad to own them, even
though I have read three of them already. I started
reading the fourth book, Prince Caspian, last
night. Saturday's present was a big bag of ketchup
chips, my favourite. The note said to share them
with Dad, and not to stay up too late. Sunday's
present was an Archie comic book.

February 25

Some people are really carrying this backwards
day thing way too far. Thomas and Nick zipped
each other's jackets on backwards at recess time.
Maggie is wearing all her clothes backwards and
is walking backwards. Adrianna has her glasses
tied on so that they stay on the back of her head.

I just wore my Blue Jays cap backwards. I am not willing to bump into things or to ask other people to dress me.

My present yesterday was a cake mix. Mom said to read the directions carefully, use the bundt pan, and get Dad to take it out of the oven for me. Luckily I knew what a bundt pan was because Dad sure wouldn't. Mom always makes her apple cinnamon coffee cake in the bundt pan. I made the cake for our supper. It wasn't too bad. Dad said he would help me make frosting for it, but I thought he had enough to do with making us grilled cheese sandwiches and opening a can of soup.

February 26

I practised my piano for twice as long as usual last night. The present I opened after school yesterday was a small wind-up toy piano. Mom's note said, "Don't forget to practice." It is like she can read my mind all the way from Halifax.

Today is crazy hat day. Maggie said there was nothing crazy about a plain old Blue Jays cap. I told her you can't always tell by the way a person looks whether they are crazy or not and it is the same with a hat. She didn't know what to say because I think she thought I was talking about her.

I finally remembered to get Dad to sign the

permission slip for the trip on Friday. He never remembers to look in my agenda. He said that he wouldn't be able to drive. I know he has missed a lot of work because of Corey so I didn't even ask him.

I heard him talking to Mom on the phone last night after I was in bed. I wish she had called earlier so that I could have talked to her. I think Mom must have been doing most of the talking because I couldn't hear Dad say anything except for "I know, Hon" a couple of times and then telling her everything would be OK but he didn't sound like he really believed it.

February 27

I am driving tomorrow with Holly's Dad. He can take four kids, counting Holly. He can't stay for the whole time so her Aunt Susan is going to pick us up to bring us back to the school. We get to be away almost the whole day. We leave right after French class, and we get back just in time for the buses. It snowed quite a bit last night, which will make the sliding even better.

My present last night was a pair of double-knit mittens, and they have real sheep's wool knit into the inside. They are really warm and don't get wet very fast. Mom knew I would need warm mittens for the winter trip. Wearing them will be the next best thing to having her with me.

I am wearing my Blue Jays cap for sports day. I also have Corey's Toronto Maple Leafs jersey on. It seems it's all about the Toronto teams with Corey. It made me sad this morning when I looked at myself in the mirror. I wish Corey was at school proudly wearing his own Toronto team stuff.

We finished reading *Roll of Thunder, Hear My Cry*. I didn't like the ending one little bit.

I won't be writing in this journal until after the March break. I have to spend the days at Grammie's. I wish Corey was not in the hospital and that we were going to Aunt Rachel's for the week like we always do during March break. I wish I hadn't complained so much last year when I wanted to go away with Holly's family instead of going with Mom and Corey. I wish it was last year or maybe next year and then Corey would be all better. I wish a lot of things, but like Mom says, "Wishing doesn't make it so."

March

March 10

Corey and Mom came home yesterday. Dad and I drove down to Halifax on Saturday to get them. Corey was sitting on a big reclining chair in the playroom when we got there. I say sitting on the chair, but the cushiony arms, seat, and back of the puffy, caramel-coloured chair seemed to have swallowed Corey and the striped hospital blanket he was wrapped up in. If he hadn't been wearing his Blue Jays cap, I don't think I would have known it was him.

The doctor signed Corey out on Sunday morning. A nurse took him to the door in a wheelchair. Mom said that they always do that with patients who are leaving the hospital. I think that if people are ready to leave, they should be able to walk out themselves. I wasn't sure Corey could have walked that far, though. He looks so sick to me. I knew he would still have no hair but I thought maybe he would look better after being there that long and getting all that treatment. But he looks worse. He is a funny colour. I know that sounds awful, but his skin looks a different colour.

We had a really good time before March break on our trip to Mrs. M.'s house. All the groups got their fires going. My group didn't win, but ours was the best for cooking, and a lot of people ended up cooking their hot dogs at our fire. Mrs. M.'s dog Sam had a wonderful time. He was constantly running after sticks and had lots of dropped hot dogs to eat. Mrs. M. said this morning that Sam slept practically the whole March break after the day he had with us. We went in to Mrs. M.'s house for cookies and hot chocolate. She called two groups in at a time. She has a big kitchen, but it would be too crowded to have the whole class in all at once. On the wall by the back door there was a picture frame with about twenty photographs in the frame. All the photographs were of Zachary. I stood there as long as I could to look at those pictures. There were more pictures of him in the kitchen and a picture of him on the fridge. I heard Mrs. M. tell one of the parents that the picture on the fridge was taken when Zac was making porridge. He was holding his little brother with one arm and stirring a pot on the stove with the other. I kept thinking about Zac being a brother. There were lots of pictures of him with his sister and two brothers. In one of the pictures he was blowing out candles on his birthday cake, and the other kids were standing behind him. Megan had her arm around him. I have thought a lot about how Mrs. M. must feel about losing Zachary, but I kept thinking while I sat there with my cup of hot chocolate about Megan, Chapin, and Caleb. Their brother died. They don't have their brother anymore. I was glad when the next group got called in, and we had to quickly finish eating and get dressed to go back out. I think if I had stayed in that kitchen much longer I would have started bawling my stupid head off.

Twenty presents took me right up to the day we drove home from Halifax. I think it's amazing that Mom guessed the exact number of days she would be gone. My last present was a camera. I opened it before we left in the morning. A real camera of my very own. The note said, "Picture this! Picture your Mom and brother back home."

March 12

Mrs. M. started reading us a book called *Number the Stars*. The story takes place in Denmark in 1943. German soldiers are patrolling the streets.

The main characters are Annemarie and her friend Ellen. Ellen is Jewish. This is a very serious book, and just like when we read *Roll of Thunder* Mrs. M. is going to let us ask questions and talk about some of the really serious or upsetting parts.

My March writing goal is conventions. That is a fancy word for remembering to use capital letters, putting in the correct punctuation, and using paragraphs and stuff. Mrs. M. says that I am already good at that but I will be extra careful in my writing this month.

We got our report cards yesterday and we have Friday off for parent-teacher meetings. Mom and Dad thought my report card was very good. Corey didn't get a report card because he has only been at school for one week all term.

March 13

Yesterday, right at the beginning of math class, Mrs. M. started to cry. We already had our math books out and she was at the board ready to teach the lesson when she just started crying. I remember thinking, "What is it about this math lesson that is making her so sad?" She had seemed fine just a second ago when she told us to open to page 157. When she spoke, her voice was very low but by that time her tears had everyone's attention and there was not a sound in the room. "I am not leaving," she said. "We are not going to go get anyone. I am going to stop crying and I need you all to help me. I want you to start the subtraction questions on page 92. I am going to pull myself together, and when I can, I am going to teach today's lesson."

She went over to her desk and sat down. No one said that we had already done the questions on page 92. As we started copying the subtraction questions into our books, Mrs. M. sobbed. The sound of her sobbing was at first enough for us to know that she wasn't ready to get back up and teach, but as a few moments went by and the crying got calmer, heads slowly bobbed up between copying and subtracting to see how she was making out pulling herself together. I had nine questions done when she stood back up and walked to the front of the room. We closed our notebooks and sat up straight as Mrs. M. began a lesson on improper fractions.

Toward the end of the class Mrs. M. stopped us and said, "Thank you so much for helping me this morning. With your help I got through without having to go home or having to get someone to come in."

She explained how the sadness sometimes comes over her like a wave, and I completely understood what she was saying. When I swim in the lake on a really windy day and the water is rough, I'll be floating on my back like I always do and a wave will suddenly come over my face. I spit and sputter, turn over quickly, and work at getting my breath back. I understand sadness, too. When I look at Corey it makes me feel so sad. I want him to be like he was, and I want to feel like I used to feel. I want to tease him, tickle him, and get mad at him. I want him to just be him and me to just be me.

March 17

Last night I looked through a pile of pictures that Mom took last summer. I found one of Corey and me at the lake. I put it in the frame on my dresser that had my soccer picture in it. I am going to look at that picture every night and imagine us at the lake this summer. I am going to imagine Corey being taller, his hair sticking out like it used to when he toweled it dry. I am going to imagine him racing me to the raft and him beating me. I am going to imagine him pushing me off the ladder, then cannonballing me. When I get to the surface Mom will be hollering at him, and I will get him back when he least expects it. Next summer I really hope that those dumb lightning bolt swimming trunks don't fit him anymore.

March 18

Corey had a really bad nosebleed last night and Mom and Dad had to take him to the hospital. Grammie came over and stayed all night with me. Corey had to stay at the hospital and Mom stayed with him. They might have to stay for a couple of days. Dad said that Corey needed a platelet transfusion and that they have to watch him for a few days to make sure that his platelets come up. I had no idea what a platelet was when Dad told me that this morning. I asked Mrs. M. what a platelet was and she let me go on the computer during roll call. There was a website called About Platelets and I went on that first. It showed a row of platelets. They looked to me like pink, five-legged, long-tailed goats lying on their backs. Platelets are something in our blood that makes it clot or get sticky when we get cut or start bleeding for some reason. Being sick or taking certain kinds of medicine can make it so that we don't have enough platelets, and then the bleeding will not stop like it is supposed to when the air hits it. Corey's platelets are too low because of the chemotherapy medicine. The doctors had to give him platelets through a tube. It showed bags of platelets on the website. They looked like yellow applesauce.

I asked Mrs. M. if I could call my grandmother at recess time. I wanted to ask her if she could take me to the hospital after school. I know Grammie is nervous driving in the city, but I couldn't stop thinking about Corey not being able to stop bleeding. I started to cry as soon as Grammie answered, and I could tell she was really worried when she heard me. I felt embarrassed standing in the office across the room from the school secretary who I am normally scared to death of, but I couldn't help myself. She was really nice, though, and came over and handed me a box of Kleenex. Grammie said to come home on the bus and she would call Dad at work. We could go meet him at his office and drive in to the hospital with him. I felt a bit better after that.

March 20

I stayed home yesterday. Grammie didn't wake me up for school and it was after 11:00 when I woke up. At first I thought it was Saturday, but then I remembered it was a school day. I also remembered my nightmare and Grammie coming into my room in the night. Everybody was bleeding. I can't remember it all now like I could when I first woke up. Grammie stayed with me. She fell asleep before I did. I just lay there in the dark, afraid to go back to sleep.

March 25

Corey's blood count came back up, and they let him come home yesterday. Uncle Paul was at our house when we got back from the hospital and he brought a Dairy Queen ice cream cake. It had a whale on it and said, "Have a whale of a time." I don't think Uncle Paul came up with that; I think he just grabbed a cake out of the display case. A whale of a time we did not have. Dad carried Corey in from the car and laid him on the couch. Mom had been crying all the way home and she went right to her room. Dad and Uncle Paul went to the basement. Later at suppertime Corey was asleep. The rest of us ate some kind of casserole from the freezer and nobody talked. I took my piece of cake to my room.

It startled me when I heard Dad holler, "What would you do that for?"

Uncle Paul told Dad that he had called their father. Dad was really mad about that. "I thought he should know about Corey," Uncle Paul said. Dad screamed that he didn't deserve to know anything about us. Dad left and slammed the door. When I went in to the kitchen, Mom was crying and Uncle Paul was hugging her. I turned around quickly so they wouldn't see me.

March 26

Dad went over to Uncle Paul's apartment last night. I heard Mom tell Dad to go talk to him, but I don't know if they are friends again. I know that sounds kind of stupid because they are brothers. But they are best friends, too. I didn't ask Dad any questions this morning, and he and Mom didn't say anything about it.

I wrote my nightmare down in my home journal. It isn't as scary to think about it now. I know that I dreamt about blood because I was thinking about Corey. In my dream everyone was bleeding, not all at the same time, but each time I saw someone they were bleeding. Holly had cut her arm on the playground, and it wouldn't stop bleeding. I ran to get the duty teacher, and when I came back, Holly was leaning against the bike rack and there was a huge puddle of blood beside her. Corey has to go every few days to get his blood taken. They have to check his white blood count, his hemoglobin, and his platelets.

March 27

I walked down to the lake after school yesterday. It is still completely frozen, but Dad says that the ice is rotten. I put my foot on the edge, but I didn't walk out on it. The ice looks really cloudy and grey, and the lake looks like a sad and lonely place. I didn't stay there very long because it made me feel that way, too.

March 28

I am so excited for my birthday. Aunt Rachel, Uncle Richard, and Zachary are coming for the weekend. Grammie and Uncle Paul will be at my birthday supper, too. I am going to have two birthday cakes because Mom is making my confetti cake and Grammie is making a chocolate cake. Dad and Uncle Paul are OK now. They went to Princess Auto together last night and then came back to work on Dad's four wheeler in our garage. When I went out to say goodnight to Dad, they were laughing, so I don't think Dad is mad at him anymore.

April

April 2

I got a lot of presents for my birthday. I also got about sixty dollars. I am ten years old, finally in the double digits. Aunt Rachel gave me ten dollars, and I got a present from Zachary, too.

Aunt Rachel, Uncle Richard, and Zachary are coming back for Easter in a couple weeks. We always have a huge Easter egg hunt. I always try to race Corey for them and it can get a little rough. This year we will have to do it differently. I think we should divide up the rooms evenly. Corey can look in the rooms that are his, and I will look in the rooms that are mine. That way I won't knock into him or hurt him in any way. If he doesn't feel like searching all his rooms, I will do it for him and give him the eggs. We never find them all right away. I remember one year I found one when we moved the couch over to make room for the Christmas tree. It was wrapped in foil so it was still good to eat.

Dad got a letter from his father. I know it was from his father because his name and return address were in the corner of the envelope. Dad acted like he wasn't going to open it, but Mom made him. The letter made my Dad cry. It made him mad, too, I think, because he was in a really bad mood afterwards.

Zachary is adorable. He smiles and laughs when you talk to him. Aunt Rachel sings to him all the time. She sings "The Happy Wanderer" to him. I learned that song at camp last year. She changed it, though, and instead of "Valderee, valderah" she sings "Zacharee, Zachara, Zacharee, Zachara, Zachara-ha-ha-ha-ha-ha, Zacharee, Zachara, my knapsack on my back." Zachary loves it.

Mrs. M. talked about the writing contest for Canadian Book Week today. She wants us all to enter a piece of writing. We all have developing a good copy for the contest as our April writing goal. She talked about me winning last year. I think it was hard for her to bring it up because it is getting really close to the time last year when Zachary died. She went on to say that she was not going to be in school the week after next. She is planning on staying home that week. April 18th will be the first-year anniversary of Zachary's death. Her voice cracked a bit and her eyes filled with tears but she was OK. She said that our stories had to be passed in for the contest by April 12th and that she would conference anyone who wanted help getting their stories ready.

I think I will enter one of the stories I wrote earlier this year. I am going to get Mrs. M. to help me decide which one and if I should add or change anything to the story I decide to enter.

April 3

I read part of my journal entry out loud to the class yesterday. I left out the part about Dad crying and being mad after getting the letter. I almost didn't read about the Zacharee song because of Mrs. M., but I did read it. Mrs. M. liked that part and told us about singing to her kids. She said that she had a song for each one of them. She used to sing "How Much Is That Doggy in the Window?" to Caleb. "I'm Going to Bop with My Baby All Night Long" was the song she sang to Chapin, and "Put Your Head on My Shoulder" was what she sang to Megan. The song she used to sing to Zachary when he was little was "Hit the Road, Jack," except she sang "Hit the road, Zac."

Some kids told about real or made-up songs that their Moms or Dads sing to them. Dad sings a lot, but I don't think he ever made up songs just for us. Lately he is stuck on singing "Get the Party Started."

I am going to enter "Mystery at Cabin Cove" in the writing contest. I changed a few things and added more detail. I think I am a better writer than I was in September. Mrs. M. says that we get better at everything the more we do it. I guess that is true.

April 4

Corey has to go back in to the hospital next week for more chemotherapy medicine. He cried last night when Mom told him. That was the first time since this all started that I have seen him cry. He was on his bed crying and yelling that he wasn't going. He didn't care what the doctors said; he wasn't going back to the hospital. I went and got the lake picture, lay down on the bed beside him, and passed him the frame. He stopped crying and looked at the picture. I told him he had to go to the hospital so that he would get better. I told him that it will be summer in three months, and he had to get the treatment over with so that we could hang out at the lake every single day. We would swim all day and forget about all the hospital stuff. I said, "Imagine that we run in the water, start swimming, get to the ladder at just about the same time, and you push me out of the way, climb up, put your arms in the air, and declare yourself the Walton Lake Champion."

We lay there for a long time not saying anything, and then he asked me if he could take the picture to the hospital with him.

April 7

Mrs. M. finished reading *Number the Stars* today. It took longer to read this book because we talked a lot about it every day. We learned a lot about the Holocaust and the way Jews were treated. Mrs. M. told us about concentration camps. She told us about some of the terrible things that were done there. She told us some stories about people who survived and about the strength and hope that people held on to. She read us a story about butterflies from another book. She didn't tell us the name of the book, but I could see that the title was *On Children and Death*. Children in the concentration camps would scratch little butterflies on the walls before entering the gas chambers. Like a butterfly emerging from a cocoon, they would emerge free into a land where there is no pain, into a land of peace and love. Mostly everyone cried when she finished reading that part.

April 8

My grandfather Leonard Broderson called last night. That's what he said when I answered the phone. "This is your grandfather, Leonard Broderson." I thought that was weird that he told me his first and last name. Then he asked me what my name was. That is weird, too, that my own grandfather had to ask me what my name was. Mom and Dad weren't home because they had to take Corey to the hospital last night so that the nurses could do some things to get Corey ready for his treatment today.

Grammie came over to stay with me until Dad got back. My grandfather asked me a lot of questions and I answered the ones I could. "Did your father get the letter I wrote him?" I said yes he did, but I did not say that it made him mad and made him cry. "How old is your little brother?" "How old are you?" "What time will your father be home?"

I told him it would be really late. I didn't think Dad would want to talk to him. My grandfather Leonard Broderson told me to get a pen and paper and write his phone number down. He talked to me like I was a little kid who couldn't figure out for myself what to do when someone was leaving a message and their phone number. When I hung up I took the page off of Mom's "Emily's Things to Do" notepad where I had copied the number and took it to my room. I put it under my pillow. I don't know why under my pillow; I just didn't want Dad to see it. I wish Mom was going to be home tonight to give it to him and talk him into calling, but I will have to tell Dad tomorrow in case Leonard Broderson calls back.

April 9

Mrs. M. brought in a picture of the headstone at Zachary's grave. She told us why she had chosen the picture that is on the headstone. The picture is of trees and two people in a canoe. She said she knew as soon as she saw that picture in the book that the man who was selling the monuments showed her, that that was exactly what she wanted at Zachary's grave. She said she really thought that the front person in the canoe looked like Zac, and she thought that the back person could be his grandfather or any one of the other people he had ever canoed with. She put his name, birthdate, and the date of his death on the headstone. She put his parents' names, and the names of his sister and two brothers. She said she did that because she wanted people to always know that he was part of a family and that he was remembered and missed by them all.

We started reading the book *Where the Red Fern Grows* today. It was written by the same author as The *Summer of the Monkeys*. The author started the story with a grown man coming upon two dogs fighting. The dogs fighting brought back memories of his childhood. He broke up the fight and took one of the dogs home to clean him up and feed him. After letting the dog go, he looked at two trophy cups on his mantel. He started telling the story of those cups and the dog, wanting memories of his childhood.

I gave Dad the paper with my grandfather's phone number on it. He put it in his pocket and didn't say anything. The phone rang twice last night and both times I answered it, I was sure that it would be Leonard Broderson. The first call was Aunt Rachel and the second one was Mom. I wonder how many days my grandfather will wait before he calls back.

April 10

We made Ukrainian Easter eggs yesterday. It was really hard to do. We used wax and a little tool called a kistka or stylus. We used a candle to melt the wax. Maggie's was the best. She is really artistic, but I would never tell her that. She knows it herself anyway.

Uncle Paul brought Chinese food for our supper last night. He bought five combos. I guess he wanted to make sure we had enough food. I ate some rice, an egg roll, and six chicken balls. They are my favourite. For me it is all about the red sauce. We ate in the family room on the TV tables. We didn't even have the TV on so I'm not sure why we didn't eat in the kitchen. Dad told Uncle Paul that their father had called him on Sunday night, but Uncle Paul already knew, which didn't make Dad very happy. From what Uncle Paul said it seems like he has been talking to my grandfather a lot lately. When he asked Dad if he was going to return his call, Dad did not answer him.

"Give the guy a break," Uncle Paul said and that made Dad even madder. After that they didn't talk about my grandfather anymore. They went to the kitchen and loaded more Chinese food on their plates and turned on the TV to some sports channel. I went to my room and wrote in my home journal. I made a list of questions that I would ask Leonard Broderson if I called him. I came up with fourteen questions. Then I wrote ten things I would tell him. By the end I was crying and I don't know why. I don't even know him and I don't know why I care if he knows us or not.

Ten things I would tell my grandfather:

1. I love to swim

2. my Mom's name is Emily

3. my Dad calls me Toad

4. Corey loves beavers

5. I have read fifteen books since Christmas

6. I like to write stories

7. Corey is sick

8. I feel guilty because I am not sick

9. We used to have a dog named Bud

10. Dad cries and gets mad when he talks about you

I would not really tell him #8. I wouldn't tell any-one that. I wouldn't tell him #10 either.

April 11

The snow is pretty much all gone. I can see a little bit at the edge of the woods behind our house but the fields are totally clear. We drove by the lake after supper last night and the thin ice has pulled away from the shore. Dad says it will be gone in a few days if the weather stays warm. The water is so high you can't see the rock on the shore where we always throw our towels. It is getting a lot warmer and I am going to ask Mom if I can stop wearing my winter coat. I don't think

Dad even knows where Mom keeps our out-of-season clothes. I think my spring jacket is hanging in the back closet. I know Mom would wash it before she would let me wear it, even though she washed it just before she put it away.

Grammie is staying with me tonight because Dad has to go to Moncton for work. She will probably clean the house as soon as she gets here because she will think it is messy. Dad and I have done our best, but I know it is a lot messier than when Mom is home. We have not eaten at the kitchen table at all this week, and it is covered with mail, newspapers, and stuff. My agenda was buried for two days, and it was just a fluke that I found it this morning when I pushed some stuff over to set my cereal bowl down.

Mrs. Scott is going to teach us next week. Mrs. M. doesn't want her to read *Where the Red Fern Grows* to us. She will probably read us ghost stories anyway. Mrs. M. read the part today where Billy gets his dogs. He cut two slits in a feed sack and put the dogs in it. They stuck their heads out through the holes. He called the puppies Old Dan and Little Ann.

We had a fire drill before recess. Nick was in his sock feet and the ground was really muddy. Mrs. M. hollered at him because he didn't have his indoor shoes on. It seemed like we were outside for a long time before Mr. Caines made the announcement for everyone to go back in. Some of the little kids in Miss Elliot's class were crying because they thought it was a real fire. I was looking at her lineup wishing that Corey was there. He has only been at school for one week since Christmas, and it doesn't look like he will get back anytime soon. The kids in his class look so much bigger than he does. Tyler could knock him over for a joke. I wonder if the kids in his class ever think about him.

Everybody passed in their piece of writing for the contest. We read them aloud to the class before we passed them in. Troy wrote a story about the character Matthew Cuthbert from *Anne of Green Gables*. It was a really good story that he made up about Matthew and his team of horses getting lost in a winter storm. Holly wrote a story about a stuffed kangaroo that takes a trip to Australia. Thomas's story was really dumb and didn't make any sense at all. Next Thursday we will have an assembly and find out who the winner will be.

April 22

We did not write in our journals at all last week so I have a lot to write about today. I know I won't

remember everything about last week, but I will
try to write about the important stuff. Sometimes
I try to write as fast as I think, but my hand gets
too tired and I give up. I am really glad Mrs. M.
is back. I saw the thing, a memorial Mom said it
was, that she put in the paper for Zachary on April
18th. The memorial said something about tears
flowing, and when I read it I thought about all the
times I have seen Mrs. M.'s tears flow.

Troy won first place in the writing contest.
Natalie Seely came in second, and Rosalind Con-
rad came in third. They are both in Grade Five.
I got an honorable mention. I was happy about
that, and I wasn't surprised because I didn't think
my story was as good as the one I wrote last year.
Even if it only got honorable mention, my story
still gets put in the binder in the library.

Mom and Corey came home on Wednesday. We
had a busy Easter weekend. Zachary is three
months old now. He laughed right out loud.

My grandfather has called a few times since I
wrote in my journal last. The first time he called I
answered, and Dad picked up the basement phone
at the same time. I hung up quickly but sat at the
top of the basement stairs so that I could hear
what Dad was saying. I didn't hear much, though,
because my grandfather was doing most of the

talking. Dad said "yeah" a lot as if he was agreeing with everything his father was saying to him.

Mrs. M. told us today that the principal from the high school called her yesterday and asked her to speak to the students at an assembly. She started to cry when she was talking and didn't say anything more. I don't know what they want her to talk about.

April 25

Zachary was drinking and driving. Mrs. M. said that this morning and said that was why they have asked her to speak to the students at the high school. She told us that she decided to do it because she thinks it is important to talk about it and tell Zachary's story. She will be going to the high school on May 2nd. That day the RCMP will be staging a mock accident where students will act out being injured and killed in a drinking and driving accident. Afterwards Mrs. M. will talk in an assembly. She said she has to get herself ready and find the right words to say to those kids. Mrs. M. was talking very quietly and her head was down. She looked up at us, and her eyes were filled with tears. The bell rang, but nobody got up until she finally smiled and moved toward the door. When I walked by her, I wanted to tell her how brave I think she is, but I didn't.

Aunt Rachel is coming today. She is staying for a week. Sunday will be Mom and Dad's anniversary. Dad had to talk Mom into going away. She didn't want to go and leave Corey. Dad called Aunt Rachel and asked her to come and when Mom knew that she was coming, she agreed to go for one night. Aunt Rachel convinced her to go for two nights. They are going to Fredericton, I think. I am really excited to see baby Zachary.

April 28

Aunt Rachel said that we need a girls' night out so tonight she, Mom, and I are going to the mall and out for supper. Dad will be home with Corey and Zachary. I don't think he will change Zachary's diaper unless he gets really wet or really stinky. Mom said he always tried to get out of changing us.

Mom called from the hotel last night. They were just going to the pool and the hot tub. They had supper at a fancy restaurant. It is their fourteenth anniversary. Mom looked so beautiful in her wedding pictures. Dad didn't have a mustache then and his face looked so skinny.

On Friday when Aunt Rachel came she cried when she saw Corey. She tried not to show it, but I

135

could see her tears when she hugged Mom. I know he is really sick. He seems to be getting weaker. He has the lake picture on his bedside table, but we don't talk about it. There are only about two months left before swimming time, and he does not seem to be getting any stronger.

April 29

We finished reading *Where the Red Fern Grows* yesterday. I couldn't write about it yesterday because it was so sad. We were all crying our heads off. We cried right up to lunchtime, and we looked like a bunch of red-faced crybabies going to the cafeteria. A couple of the kids had to stay in the classroom to eat their lunch with Miss Reinhart because they couldn't stop crying. I really loved the book, but I don't know if I would have wanted to hear the story if I had known how sad it was at the end.

I got a new pair of jeans and a new jacket on our girls' night out yesterday. We ate at Pizza Delight. I got the quarter chicken dinner. It was really good. Dad had changed Zachary when we got home, and he and Zachary and Corey were sleeping on the family room couch. The dirty diaper was still on the floor.

April 30

Mom and Corey have to go to Halifax on Friday. Mom told me last night that Corey will be having more radiation and chemotherapy and that they might start harvesting Corey's stem cells. I really didn't understand what Mom was telling me. What I do understand is that Corey is not getting better. I also understand that my family is not getting back to normal and that this is not going away. I wanted to put my fingers in my ears when she was talking. I wanted to scream and stamp my feet. I wanted to have a major temper tantrum, and I wanted that temper tantrum to make this all go away. If throwing a fit would make this all go away, I would throw one huge fit, screaming my head off, holding my breath until I fell over, kicking my feet and thrashing my arms. I would even beat my head against the floor. I would throw one gargantuan fit if doing that would make this all go away. But it is not going away, and I have to do my best to pretend that I believe everything will be all right. I seem to be getting quite good at that. I am just as good as Mom and Dad and almost as good as Corey. He is the best actor of us all.

May

May 1

Mrs. M. is reading *Holes* to us. Stanley Yelnats is the main character. His name is a palindrome. My name would be Taylor Rolyat if it was a palindrome. Corey's would be Corey Yeroc. Thomas's would be Thomas Samoht.

Mrs. M. won't be here tomorrow. She is going to be at the high school. Mrs. Shannon is going with her. She told us that if she starts talking and gets too emotional and can't keep going that Mrs. Shannon is going to finish for her. I think that she will be able to do it herself. She has talked to us a lot of times, started crying, and then pulled herself together. It will be hard to speak to a whole school, though.

I started a story at home on our computer. I am going to try to write a little bit on it every day. It doesn't have a title yet. My main character's name is Lily. She has to go live with her grandfather after her parents die in a car accident. She has never met him before.

May 6

I spent the weekend at Grammie's. She gets the newspaper and she showed me the picture that was taken at the high school on Friday. They had two smashed-up cars, and kids were lying on the ground, and one guy was lying on the hood of one of the cars. It was a pretend accident, but it looked real. Mrs. M.'s name was in the write-up underneath it. It told about her speaking to the students about her son's death in a drinking and driving accident. I wonder if she will say anything about it to us. I don't think I should ask her how she made out. Holly brought the picture in, but I told her not to show it to Mrs. M. I'm sure she has probably seen it, but I don't think she should be made to talk about it if she doesn't want to.

I hate it when people think they have to talk to me about Corey. At Grammie's on Sunday afternoon, her neighbour Mrs. Kingsley came over for tea. She gushed all over me and kept asking me questions about Corey. "You poor dear," she kept saying between questions. "You poor dear," and "God love you." I stood there politely, gritting my teeth until Grammie finally asked me to get them some hot tea. I poured their tea and left the room as quickly as I could. I stayed away until she was gone. I don't know what to say to people.

Dad got home last night but it was late so I stayed at Grammie's. She drove me home this morning in time for me to catch the bus. She is going to stay with us this week because Dad has to be away two nights for work and he might have to work late, too. We are going to go to Halifax on the weekend.

May 8

It is raining really hard and we just had an indoor recess. I tried to read, but Thomas and Nick kept bugging me. I hope it stops raining before I get home. I want to go biking. Yesterday I rode to the lake and sat on the towel rock. It is almost completely out of the water. I had been feeling so alone, but sitting at the lake I felt like I was with Mom and Corey. I squeezed my eyes tightly and pretended that I could hear splashing and laughing and both of their voices. As long as I could keep my eyes closed I could keep them there.

May 9

Dad is picking me up at lunchtime today. He told me to eat in the cafeteria and then wait in the office for him. We are going to Halifax. I packed a few things this morning. I don't know why I didn't pack anything last night. Dad kept telling

me to, but I couldn't make myself. I told him when
he tucked me in that I was all packed, and I had
Mom's small suitcase on the floor at the foot of my
bed so that Dad would think that I had. I want to
go see Mom and Corey, but I don't want to go. Last
night, each time I thought about putting stuff in
the suitcase I would start to feel like I was going
to cry so I would quickly start doing something
else. I even cleaned my whole closet to give me
something else to do. I just threw clean underwear, my bathing suit, Erno and Bartholomew,
and about ten books in the suitcase this morning
and put it by the front door for Dad to put in the
car before I ran to catch the bus.

I went for a ride by the lake two nights ago and
I didn't even stop. I sped up when I got close to
it and rode as fast as I could when I got right up
to it. I turned my head and didn't even look at
the part of the shore where we swim. On the way
back I almost stopped, but instead I pretended I
was in a race and that I was leading everyone by
so much that the people behind me were not even
in sight. I didn't stop until I got to the top of the
hill around the turn where you can't even see the
lake. I decided to wait 68 (my favourite number)
days before I went by the lake again. I would keep
count of the days on a kitten calendar Grammie

gave me for my birthday. I would not count ahead to see where 68 days takes me. Each day I would put the letters NL1, NL2, and so on until I get to NL68. NL stands for No Lake.

When I get to NL68, I believe Corey will be better and we will swim from 10:00 in the morning until 4:00 in the afternoon. I will make Corey's favourite sandwiches—peanut butter and Fluff—and we will have a picnic on the shore. Even if it is pouring rain on day 68 we will swim and have our picnic. I am not going to tell anyone until the morning of day 67 so Mom can buy some Fluff and make the plans to spend the whole day at the lake. 68 days. If I can go 68 days without going by the lake, Corey will get better.

Today I put NL2, NL3, and NL4 on the calendar. I know I will not see the lake on the weekend because we will be in Halifax. I think the reason I don't want to go to Halifax is because I am afraid to see Corey. I am afraid that when I see him I will not be able to believe he will be all better by day 68.

May 20

I don't care that I missed a whole week of school. I don't care that I missed Kayla's birthday party. Mrs. M. said I could write the math test I missed tomorrow. I don't care. I don't care that I missed hearing most of the book *Holes*. My book order came in while I was gone but I don't care. I didn't even look at the books when Mrs. M. gave them to me. I just put them in my book bag. I don't care about anything. I don't care about writing in my journal either. I might just draw a picture of Thomas's big old ugly butt. I might see how many times I can write "I don't care" before Mrs. M. tells us to stop writing. Then I might just stand up and tell everyone how much I don't care, and I might just use the "f" word like Dad did when we got to the hospital.

May 21

Last night I wrote 45 Reasons Why This Is NOT Fair in my home journal. I only stopped at 45 because Grammie made me turn out my light. I didn't even put the journal away. I slid it under my pillow when she opened the door. I hadn't brushed my teeth. I hadn't even put on my pyjamas but I pulled the blankets up to my chin, and Grammie didn't know. She asked me if I wanted to talk, but I told her I was tired and wanted to get to sleep.

I wrote my math test at recess. I put down all wrong answers on purpose. What difference does a math test make? What difference does anything make?

I tore up all the pages of the stupid kitten calendar Sunday when I got home. The stupid kitten calendar and the stupid idea that Corey would get better in 68 days. Instead Mom told us as soon as we got to the hospital that Corey has to go to Toronto to the Hospital for Sick Children to have a stem cell transplant. Then he has to come back to Halifax. I couldn't believe it when Mom said six weeks in Toronto and eight weeks in Halifax. Six and eight. I am so stupid. How could I think 68 days would be enough to make Corey all better?

6 x 7 is 42 and 8 x 7 is 56 and 42 + 56 = 98 days and before I tore up the calendar I counted 98 days and we probably won't be able to swim on September 25.

May 22

Dad was mad at me when he realized that I hadn't packed any pyjamas, no clean clothes, and no toothbrush or toothpaste for the weekend. Then when we ended up staying all week, he was even more annoyed. We had to go to the nearest Wal-Mart and buy some stuff. Dad doesn't like to shop, and he doesn't like the Wal-Mart. Mom would have checked. She would have looked in my suitcase or laid some stuff out for me to pack. But Mom wasn't there and she won't be there for a long time. I know that she is sorry about that, and I know that there is nothing she can do about it. But I need her, too. I wanted to tell her that. I felt like crying and begging her to please come home and that I need her, too. I would never say that in front of Corey. Corey was so weak and looked so sick that he didn't even seem to notice that Dad and I were there and didn't seem to hear anything we were saying. He has sores in his mouth, Mom said, and they hurt so much that he doesn't even try to talk. Mom says he has the sores because his blood counts are so low. She has to rinse out his mouth with a solution several times a day. He doesn't like this and she can barely get him to open his mouth.

May 27

Mom called from Toronto last night. She is staying in a place called the Residence College Hotel. It is for the relatives of patients, and it is right across the street from the hospital so she can walk back and forth. She goes to the hospital early in the morning and leaves at about 10:00 at night if Corey is sleeping. She says that he is sleeping almost all the time.

Mrs. M. gave me another copy of the math test before roll call question today. She told me she knew that my mind wasn't on it when I did it last week, and that I should try it again and take as long as I needed to come up with the right answers. She said she understood how sometimes when something really hurts, other things don't seem to matter. I did my best and I think I got most of the questions right. Some teachers would just have marked everything wrong and not cared, but not Mrs. M.

May 28

My grandfather called last night. He asked Dad if it would be all right if he went to the hospital to see Mom and Corey. It would be to meet them really since he has never seen them before. He lives in Markham, which is close to Toronto, Dad says. Dad told him he could go see them if he wanted to. They have talked to each other a few times on the phone and I think Dad is talking nicer to him than he was at first. Later when Dad talked to Mom on the phone, I heard him give her my grandfather's phone number.

Uncle Paul took me bowling on Saturday afternoon. I think he was trying to show off for his new girlfriend. He was gushy sweet to me and bought me about a hundred treats at the bowling alley plus supper at McDonald's. Her name is Roxanne and she is really pretty. She hugged me when she met me and said how sorry she was about my brother. I hate first-meeting huggers. She was a long hugger, too. I guess Uncle Paul would like that about her, but me, not so much.

June

June 3

My grandfather called last night. I answered the phone and he talked to me a lot without even asking to talk to Dad. He has been to the hospital every day to see Mom and Corey. He said that he saw a picture of me and that I remind him of Gloria. He said "Gloria," not "your grandmother," and that sounded kind of funny to me. Then he told me that Gloria was a beautiful woman and I didn't know what to say. "You have her hair," he said. I thought about Corey with nobody's hair, not even his own. He went on to say that he was very anxious to meet me. I was very quiet for my usual chatty self and before he even asked I told him I would go get Dad. Dad told me after he got off the phone that my grandfather was coming here to see us. He is coming on June 13th.

June 5

Uncle Paul and Roxanne came for supper last night. She brought lasagna and Caesar salad. It wasn't as good as Aunt Rachel's but it was OK. She helped me empty the dishwasher and set the table before we ate. Dad and I have not eaten at the table since Mom and Corey left. It was nice to have a good supper, but I missed Mom so much. I know Dad misses her a lot, too. After supper Dad and Paul talked about their Dad coming. He will stay at our house because Uncle Paul's apartment has only one bedroom. We have a spare room in the basement, but it is really messy and doesn't have a bed in it. Dad said that he was going to buy a bed for it, and Uncle Paul said he would pick it up with his truck so that Dad wouldn't have to pay to have it delivered. Dad told Uncle Paul that he had better plan on being here most of the time that my grandfather is here because he wasn't going to entertain him by himself.

June 6

The lilac bush by the back steps is blossoming. I took a picture of it yesterday and e-mailed it to Mom. She loves her bushes and flowers. She didn't get to see the tulips and those other purple flowers that come quite a while before her other flowers. I am trying to pay attention to them for her. Dad says that we will fill the window boxes next weekend. Mom always does all the garden work; Dad just mows the lawn.

June 11

Uncle Paul brought the new bed over last night and we got the spare room all set up for my grandfather. I took one of Mom and Dad's wedding pictures out of the living room and put it on the dresser. I put some pictures of Corey and me there, too. One of the pictures shows me pulling Corey across the kitchen floor on a blanket. He is about two years old, which makes me about four. He is laughing like crazy. I remember how much he loved for me to do that. I put my Grade One picture on the dresser, too. It is in a "Schooldays" frame and my two front teeth are missing. I found my Dad's high school graduation picture. His hair was down to his shoulders. It is in a cardboard folder. I leaned it against the mirror. I thought that maybe when Dad saw it he would make me take it off, but he didn't say anything.

June 12

In one more day I will meet my grandfather. Uncle Paul, Dad, and I will pick him up at the airport in Moncton. He gets there at 11:00 at night. At first Dad wasn't going to let me come to the airport, but then he changed his mind. I think part of what changed his mind is that he wants as many people there to meet my grandfather as possible so that he won't have to do all the talking. Even though he has talked to him a lot on the phone, I know that Dad is nervous about seeing his father after all these years. I can tell when Dad is nervous about something because he gets really corny and makes dumb jokes about everything along with being snappy and sarcastic. I wish Mom was here to level him out. She is good at calming his up and down moods. I don't know how she does it or I would try to do what she does.

Roxanne is going to wait at our house because the car would be too crowded if she came. I think Uncle Paul really likes Roxanne. I hope they don't break up because I like her, too.

It has been warm enough to swim, but I try not to think about it.

June 17

My grandfather is really funny. He calls me Tator. I couldn't believe how quickly I liked him. It feels like I have known him for a long time and when he called me Tator Saturday afternoon, I didn't even mind. He taught me how to play Cribbage. I can even count my own hand now. At first I had no clue how you got points. I beat him last night.

I think my Dad looks like him, except Gramps has hardly any hair. I call him Gramps. He told me on the drive home Friday night that Corey calls him Gramps. I wasn't sure what I was supposed to call him and Gramps sounded much better than Leonard or Mr. Broderson or Dad's dad. He is staying for ten days.

June 18

I talked to Mom and Corey on the phone last night. Corey sounded pretty good. Gramps talked to them, too. He told Corey that he has learned a lot about beavers from the books in his room and that he found a couple of new sticks by the pond to add to his collection.

I can't believe that there are only one and a half more days left of Grade Four. I hope Holly, Victoria, Kayla, Adrianna, and I all get in the same class next year. I don't even care who we get for a teacher as long as we are together.

June 19

We have packed up all the things in our desks. My book bag is full and I have two plastic bags to take home. This will be the last time I will write in this journal. After we are done writing we are putting all the desks on one side of the classroom.

We will leave our chairs down for tomorrow, but we won't do any work or anything. A lot of kids aren't even coming tomorrow. I am, though, because I need one more day being in Mrs. M.'s class; one more half-day anyway. After two years it will be weird for her not to be my teacher. I will miss a whole lot of things about Grade Four.

Epilogue

September 2005

Corey died two months ago. His funeral was on a Monday and it was raining when we got back home. I stood in the backyard by myself and after several tries, I lit a fire in the outdoor fireplace. I kept adding newspaper to the wet wood until there was a bed of coals and then I set my home journal in the coals. I watched it smoulder and then finally ignite. I stood in the rain and watched it burn. On the burning pages I had written it all—all the pain, all the suffering, all the courage, all the tears, all the screaming, all the hope and the hopelessness, the waiting, the nightmares, the guilt, and the helplessness. It was a jumble of everything I had felt from the day I started writing in it. I couldn't keep it. I waited until I could not see a trace of it in the ashes before I went inside.

Yesterday I took my Grade Four journal out of the box beneath my bed. I had not looked at it since the day I put it there, on the last day of school two years ago. I set it on my bedside table and left it there for a while before I opened it. I thought of all that had happened since I wrote the last entry.

Uncle Paul and Roxanne got married last October. Corey wore a tuxedo and a really fancy top hat. He was Uncle Paul's best man. Uncle Paul said Corey was the best man he had ever met so he had to do the job. Aunt Rachel and Uncle Richard had a baby girl, Madeline. She is five months old now, and Zachary loves being a big brother. Gramps moved to Saint John to be closer to us.

I picked up the journal and read every page. Some of what I had written was embarrassing to read. I was such a little kid. I remembered how many times Mrs. M. had told us how important our journals would be to us some day. I had no desire to burn this one. I wanted to remember Grade Four and who I was before and how our family was before. But somehow it seemed that I needed to add to those pages; I needed to say who I am now and how our family is now. I didn't need to write all the things I had written and burned; I just had to tell a bit of the story so I began writing on the empty pages.

On July 5, 2005, we brought Corey home from the hospital. There was nothing more to hope for so we brought him home where he belonged.

Every day, we all went to the lake. Gramps would skip stones and Corey would count the ripples. Uncle Paul and Aunt Roxanne would pull Corey out in the dinghy and lift him onto the raft. Zachary would wear his water wings and Aunt Rachel would walk him out to his elbows. Grammie would push Madeline in her stroller back and forth on the road until she fell asleep. Mom and Dad and Uncle Richard would swim with me, and we would splash Corey when he asked us to. The splashes would soak the raft and Corey would shake his bald head and laugh.

At night we would all sit outside around the fireplace as long as we could, telling stories. Gramps had all kinds of stories about Dad when he was little and Corey seemed to like those best. We did that for twenty days. Twenty beautiful days that went so fast but will never seem like enough.

For the last two days Corey couldn't get out of bed, and a nurse came to help Mom and Aunt Rachel. Gramps barely left his side, and if he did fall asleep for a while, it was in the easy chair Dad had put beside Corey's bed. Gramps held Dad up when the end came, and I will never forget the sound of my dad's crying.

Uncle Paul and Aunt Roxanne took me for a drive so that I wouldn't have to be there when they came to take Corey. Mom and Dad went to the funeral parlour to plan Corey's funeral.

I put Corey's favourite Horrible Harry book in the casket. I also put *Danny, the Champion of the World* in. I divided a bag of Party Mix and put everything into Ziploc bags. I put them in along with one of his stuffed beavers. I didn't put in his favourite one. I wanted to keep that one myself. I know the rest put things in, too, but the only other thing I know was the copy of *Love You Forever* that Mom put in. It's not that I didn't care what the others put in. I just thought that it was between them and Corey.

I didn't have a school journal in Grade Five or Grade Six so I don't have a written record of those two years. But I kept track of how many days Corey was in the hospital during that time and it was 278 days. He never did get to go back to school.

The writer in me has a thing about giving everything I write a title and I call my Grade Four journal The Year Mrs. Montague Cried. When I think back to that year, the year Mrs. Montague cried was also the year I cried. But thanks to her I laughed a lot, too. I listened to stories and told stories of my own. I paid attention to a lot of things, and I watched how someone lets go of someone they love. I learned how to let Corey go just like Mrs. Montague let Zachary go. We let them go and keep them at the same time, and the way we keep them no one and nothing can take away from us.

I still cry and I know that I will cry for a long time, just as I know that Mrs. Montague does, but I see the crying as a gift, a gift that comes from love, a gift that Zachary and Corey gave to us when they became butterflies.

Take the **Taylor Anne Reading Challenge**,
read all the books she read in
"The Year Mrs. Montague Cried"

Danny the Champion of the World Roald Dahl

Matilda Roald Dahl

A Series of Unfortunate Events Lemony Snicket

Because of Winn Dixie Kate DiCamillo

There's a Boy in the Girl's Bathroom Louis Sachar

Anne of Green Gables Lucy Maude Montgomery

Summer of the Monkeys Wilson Rawls

The Best Christmas Pageant Ever
Barbara Robinson

The Christmas Miracle of Jonathan Toomey
Susan Wojciechowski

The Lion, the Witch and the Wardrobe C.S. Lewis

Anne of Avonlea Lucy Maude Montgomery

Anne of the Island Lucy Maude Montgomery

LPL DISCARD

Anne of Windy Poplars Lucy Maude Montgomery

Anne's House of Dreams Lucy Maude Montgomery

Anne of Ingleside Lucy Maude Montgomery

Hatchet Gary Paulsen

The Miraculous Journey of Edward Tulane
Kate DiCamillo

Willow George Lucas

A Handful of Time Kit Pearson

Love You Forever Robert Munsch

Roll of Thunder, Hear my Cry Mildred D Taylor

Song of the Trees Mildred Taylor

Where the Red Fern Grows Wilson Rawls

Number the Stars Lois Lowry

Holes Louis Sachar